Warner Books, Inc., 1271 Avenue of the Americas, New York, NY 10020

Visit our Web site at www.twbookmark.com

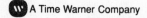 A Time Warner Company

Printed in the United States of America

First Printing: August 2000

10 9 8 7 6 5 4 3 2 1

Library of Congress Cataloging-in-Publication Data
Stone, Katherine
    Island of dreams / by Katherine Stone.
        p. cm.
    ISBN 0-446-52182-5
    1. Girls—Education—Fiction. 2. School principals—Fiction.
    3. Denver (Colo.)—Fiction. 4 Women singers—Fiction. I. Title.

PS3569.T64134 I75 2000
813'54—dc21   00-028102

KATHERINE STONE

ISLAND of DREAMS

WARNER BOOKS

A Time Warner Company

When I seek another word for music, I always find only the word Venice.

—F. W. Nietzsche
Ecce Homo

ISLAND *of* DREAMS

PROLOGUE

"*T*his is Gabriel Rourke, sir. Thank you for taking my call. I'm not certain if you remember me. It's been thirteen years."

"Remember you?" Edward Prescott was incredulous. "Not in thirteen years or thirty—not ever—will I forget you or what you did."

"Anyone would have done the same."

But no one else had. And there had been others who could have, who'd been suspicious, too.

But only the thirty-year-old immigrant from Northern Ireland had intervened.

Gabriel was a carpenter. Which was the only reason he'd been precisely where he needed to be—the Crystal Palace

1

parking lot in Greenwood Village—on that Tuesday evening in May.

The Palace, renowned for its cake-and-ice-cream creations, was undergoing a major and necessary expansion. Not only were parents who'd celebrated their childhood birthdays at the famous eatery treating their own children to such happy memories, they were scheduling extravaganzas for themselves as well, galas of calories, of nostalgia, of fun in commemoration of the Big 3-0, 4-0, 5-0.

Construction took place even as the original dining rooms remained opened, busy, full. All essential jackhammering had been accomplished outside of business hours, and thanks to a plywood partition, the sounds of hammers, drills, and saws became nonintrusive accompaniments to the sheer gaiety within.

On that May evening at quitting time Gabriel Rourke, like the rest of the crew, collected his tools, his tool belt, his lunch pail, his keys. As always Gabriel was eager to go home, to *be* home, with his beloved Eileen.

His pregnant Eileen.

So very eager to be with her. But as always Gabriel gathered his belongings methodically, moving at a pace which, had it been a minute more swift or a minute more slow, might well have cost a young girl her life.

That ten-year-old girl was on the other side of the plywood partition, and she was announcing in a most ladylike way, for Valerie Elizabeth Prescott *was* a lady, that she believed she would just scoot off for a moment to the powder room.

No further explanation was required. But Valerie embellished nonetheless, as she often did. Her fingers were sticky from the ice cream, she said. Well, she clarified, from the chocolate sauce *really*. And since the present opening was soon to begin, and she'd definitely want to touch every one of Sarah's gifts, she'd best wash the stickiness, the chocolateness, away.

Five of the eleven other girls at the birthday table accompanied her, as did two of the four moms. As chaperones? No. That thought, all four mothers subsequently confessed, hadn't crossed their minds.

The girls were ten years old and more grown up—growing up so fast!—every day. And they were in the Crystal Palace in idyllic Greenwood Village. And the short journey to the powder room was, save for a final brightly lighted hallway, entirely in plain view.

It was in the hallway that the man made his approach.

Valerie had finished washing her hands and was returning by herself to the table. She'd thought of something happy to say to Marjorie, after which she'd give her friend a hug. Marjorie needed hugs and happiness these days. Her parents' divorce had tumbled her world.

The man seemed very nice, a bewildered but not overly frightened Valerie would later assert. And definitely *not*, she would insist, a stranger—by which she meant, a definition that would become emblazoned in the hearts of parents for miles around, he wasn't *strange*. He looked familiar, usual. He reminded her, in fact, of several of her friends' fathers.

He *was* a father, or so he said. His daughters, twins

about Valerie's age, had been so thrilled with the golden retriever puppy he'd gotten for them.

The puppy, Millie, was asleep in his van and hopefully not too warm. No, don't worry, she wasn't. But the sooner he got back to her the better. With Valerie's help, he suggested, that might be very soon.

His daughters absolutely loved Millie. She was the sweetest thing. But both girls were hopelessly allergic to her fluffy fur. Millie needed a new home. There was no choice. His daughters understood, although it upset them terribly. They'd be happy again, as happy given the circumstances as they could possibly be, when they knew their father had found for Millie the very best home.

Which was why he'd brought the golden puppy to the Crystal Palace. Loving parents celebrated their children's birthdays here, just as he and his wife celebrated the twins'. Millie would make the perfect surprise present, wouldn't she?

Yes, Valerie agreed. A perfect surprise for Marjorie, she thought as she accompanied the not-strange man to his van outside. Marjorie, who was so sad.

That's all it took. It was that easy. A familiar-looking man with a smile and a puppy.

The many deceits and disguises of those who would prey on children was not—at that time—an issue on which parents were frantically focused. There'd been no need to be. Then. Although all the usual parental admonitions about "strangers" had been somberly and repeatedly shared.

And had any parent of the fourth-grade class at Hazel

Traphagen's School for Girls been asked who among the birthday celebrants was least likely to be lured by a smile-and-puppy ruse, the answer would have been a unanimous *Valerie*.

She was terribly bright, and as the only child of adoring parents, and the beloved only grandchild, too, she had a maturity beyond her years.

Valerie's mother, Lilah Carrington Prescott, was not among the mothers at the birthday party. It was a rare absence. Indeed, the girls' parents would all later reflect, it was the only birthday party anyone could remember that Lilah had ever missed.

Valerie would not have been alone in the hallway had Lilah been there. Alone anywhere, ever. Which was why Lilah wasn't at the Palace on that evening in May. She was too protective, she told herself. Too omnipresent and hovering. Not that Valerie complained. Not that anyone did.

Lilah had decided on her own that she must begin to wean herself, a gradual taper, from her precious little girl. For Valerie's sake, and her own. If she began absenting herself from a party here, a picnic there, when the time came for Valerie to spread her wings, then maybe, maybe, Lilah could survive the loss.

So Lilah wasn't at the Palace, and neither Valerie's friends nor their mothers witnessed the brief conversation or saw her leave. A few of the other patrons had noticed, they realized in retrospect. But nary a red flag had fluttered, much less waved. In this fashionable neighborhood, in this festive venue of ice cream and cake, designer-dressed fathers and daughters came and went all the time.

The parking-lot witnesses were another matter. Particularly those close enough to see the girl's expression when the man slid open the passenger-side door to create a passageway that was just wide enough for the slim girl to slip inside.

Which Valerie did. But almost didn't.

Every parking-lot witness saw her hesitation, and those closest saw her frown. And the man's answering smile. He was a handsome man. It was a convincing smile. The onlookers were convinced, permitted themselves to be, and when the man touched a finger to his smiling lips, a reminder to the girl to be very quiet, the narrow opening suddenly made perfect sense.

Someone or something was asleep inside.

The delicacy with which the man closed the door behind her further reassured the bystanders. And it wasn't really that odd, they persuaded themselves, for him to move so quickly, one might say urgently, to the driver's side.

Of all the witnesses Gabriel Rourke was farthest away. His battered-but-reliable truck was in the remote corner of the parking lot designated for those who came to the shopping center to work, not buy.

Gabriel sensed the danger right away. He was moving toward Valerie even before her momentary balk.

Gabriel's alertness to impending peril was a consequence, perhaps, of his Belfast boyhood. Wariness had been essential there; suspicion the most certain way to survive. But maybe Gabriel Rourke's ability to sense a child in jeopardy was more newly acquired. Maybe the father-to-be could perceive with brilliant clarity when a man and girl didn't belong together *at all*.

Instinct, Gabriel would later reply when asked what had guided him.

Instinct. Primal, fierce, sure. The male of the species protecting its young, even another man's young, from harm.

Gabriel reached the van just as the man was starting to open the driver's-side door.

"Stop," he commanded quietly. Primal and fierce and sure. And when the surprised man obeyed, "I want to speak with the girl."

The man's surprise shifted to panic and just enough indecision—to flee on foot or by car?—that Gabriel, not indecisive in the least, was able to grab him and hold him until help arrived . . . which it did quickly, in the form of the onlookers who'd wondered and even worried but had failed to intervene.

It would be years before the promptly freed Valerie would realize how horrific her ordeal might have been. On that evening bewilderment trumped terror.

But Valerie's parents knew. *All* the parents knew.

The man was a twice-convicted pedophile. There'd even been a death the second time. An accidental death, the felon's defense attorneys succeeded in persuading an overworked DA.

The case was pled down to involuntary manslaughter, child slaughter, for which, after an obscenely brief time behind bars, the predator was deemed rehabilitated *again* and set free.

Edward and Lilah Prescott knew on that evening what Valerie would come to know when she was older: that whether she'd have been killed in the van or dumped alive and bleeding on a roadside miles away her life had been saved by Gabriel Rourke.

Her life. And Lilah's. And Edward's.

Gabriel Rourke had saved a family.

Even then Edward Prescott had the wealth and influence to grant Valerie's savior virtually any wish. Edward wanted to. Offered to.

But the Irish carpenter declined. Solemnly. Then liltingly.

He wasn't a rich man, he admitted. "Not if it's cash you're measuring." But his glorious Eileen loved him beyond all reason, and their first child—"a boy the doctors are thinking"—would soon be born, and of all the ways a man might earn a living, he'd been lucky enough to find one that he truly enjoyed.

What more, Gabriel Rourke had wondered, could a man possibly want or need?

Nothing, Edward had known. For he, too, was blessed with a wife he loved, a daughter he cherished, and a fulfilling career.

Edward happened to have a few *other* fortunes as well, inherited and earned, which he would happily share with the man who'd saved his little girl. And should the comfortably wealthy Gabriel want to work still at his chosen career, a single phone call from Edward Prescott to Denver's premier land developer would secure a lifetime of carpentry on the highest-paying scale.

Gabriel declined. Everything. He liked the contractor for

whom he worked, and the men on the crew. The pay was fine as well, enough to support his family, which was important for him to do. On his own.

Gabriel Rourke neither needed nor wanted a benefactor. Much less, Edward realized, a guardian angel poised to swoop to the rescue should the slightest misstep occur.

Edward respected Gabriel's wishes. Respected him.

The offer stood, Edward told him. All offers stood. And always would. Gabriel merely needed to let him know.

The two men went their separate ways—although, and so discreetly that Gabriel never knew, Edward made a point of confirming that Gabriel's son arrived, healthy and fine, and that the new mother was fine and healthy, too.

Edward hadn't checked on Gabriel since.

But had he forgotten him? Never.

And now, after thirteen years, Gabriel was calling.

Edward's mind's eye saw the thirty-year-old Irishman he had known, the husband and father whose priorities had been so simple, so joyous, so clear.

And so lilting.

The sounds of Ireland, its music and its magic, were gone now from Gabriel's voice. The man who'd had very little, and everything, had lost his joy.

Had it been a sudden loss? Edward wondered. Or a relentless erosion over time, like waves upon rock, an incessant battering that rendered once proud and rugged granite docile and smooth.

Tragedy had befallen Gabriel Rourke. Edward was sure of it. Even as his own life had become even better, even happier, with each passing day.

9

The photographs in Edward's office at Prescott Bank gave glowing testimony to his many blessings. Lilah, his wife of twenty-five years, smiled at him from the walls, bookshelves, credenza, desk. As did his precious Valerie, in a kaleidoscope of joy, from infancy to girlhood to womanhood. A college graduate two years ago, last June Edward's daughter had become a bride.

Valerie's groom, Thomas Evanson, had been a medical student when they'd wed. But he'd graduated now, just, with honors from Stanford. The future neurologist would be training in Denver.

Thomas and Valerie would be arriving tomorrow in fact. *Tomorrow.* And until Christmas at least, and hopefully much longer, the couple would live with Edward and Lilah at Holly Hills.

This summer, while intern Thomas "grueled"—Valerie's word—she herself would be "gestating." Yes, she was pregnant. What *fun* she and Lilah were going to have decorating the nursery adjacent to the master suite in the mansion's east wing.

Edward Prescott was filled with the kind of joyous anticipation of new life, new love, that must have been humming within Gabriel Rourke on the evening he'd saved Edward's precious Val.

"How are you, Gabriel?"

"Fine. Good."

"And your family?" Edward queried with dread.

"Ah, they're fine, too. *Wonderful.*" The music returned. Ireland returned. "My Eileen is getting prettier by the day, and my Liam, *our* Liam, well, he's thirteen now. Becoming a man. He's the reason I'm calling. I'd like you to meet him . . . them."

"I'd love to. And if there's something else, anything else that any of you need, I do hope you'll tell me."

"There is, sir. And I will. But not, if you don't mind, until we meet."

"I don't mind in the least."

Would this coming Saturday afternoon work for him? Gabriel wanted to know. Yes, Edward replied. Saturday was good.

And would it be possible for Edward to come to the Rourkes' west Denver home?

Of course.

At, say, shortly before four?

That would be perfect, Edward said—and thought after the conversation ended. *Shortly before four* was perfect in its very imperfection, the casual imprecision that was such a sharp contrast to the financial world Edward knew, where time, which was money, was scheduled to the millisecond.

But this was Irish time. Carpenter time.

Gabriel time. Which was priceless. Peerless in its worth. For it was Gabriel time that had guided the Irish carpenter to collect his belongings at the precise pace, the perfect pace, to guarantee his arrival in the Crystal Palace parking lot at the exact millisecond necessary to save Valerie's life.

Edward very much hoped that Gabriel's favor would be substantial.

Hoped, but doubted. Gabriel would be asking for a loan at most, and more likely a referral to a higher-paying job.

The son who was becoming a man would be college-bound in no time, Gabriel would explain. A little more money in savings wouldn't hurt.

Edward could set up a college fund for Liam Rourke. Would do so happily. Edward would be delighted, for that matter, to establish such funds for every one of Gabriel's—and Liam's—heirs.

But Gabriel would decline such largesse. It was difficult enough, Edward imagined, for the proud Irishman to ask for any favor, no matter how trivial to Edward such a favor might be.

*E*dward Prescott spent the days before the Saturday afternoon visit to Gabriel's home in a swirl of sheer bliss, welcoming Valerie, welcoming Thomas, with Lilah.

And how did Gabriel Rourke spend those days?

With peace, with hope, with calm.

With song. With his Liam.

Neither father nor son had sung a note in almost three years. But following the conversation with Edward, Gabriel found his son reading in the small kitchen of their modest home.

"Sing with me, Liam."

The solemn face, so like Gabriel's own, registered surprise. "Sing with you, Da?"

There was more surprise, Gabriel noted—and such hope—when his son's dark green eyes saw his own sudden smile. "I'm wanting to hear, my boy, with your voice that's getting so deep if you still have the gift."

The gift. For music. For song. It was perfect pitch, and more. Like his father, Liam Pierce Rourke could hear music everywhere, in every spoken word, in every whispered breeze, in the hum of grass and the dance of flowers, and in sunshine, in moonlight, in the silver glow of stars.

All things can sing, Gabriel told his son, began telling him from the time Liam was very young. And all things *want* to sing. Even houses.

Houses, Da?

Especially houses, Liam. Where families live and dreams are born.

But large buildings, too, could sing, Gabriel explained. Even skyscrapers. You needed only to listen to the songs of stone, of glass, of wood, of steel while the mammoth structures were being built.

Liam inherited from his father his gift for music as surely as he inherited Gabriel's midnight black hair and dark green eyes.

And from Eileen? The mother who confessed on a laugh that she hadn't the slightest prayer of ever carrying a tune? It was Eileen's love, Eileen's joy, that enabled her son and her husband to hear the magic they did.

Sing to me, my men! she would command. And her Gabriel and her Liam would sing. And sing. And sing.

Until three years ago.

The singing stopped then, the music was no more.

But now, just days before the anniversary of that devastating day, father and son were singing anew. And they were hearing anew the music of their world.

It was a different world, a different music, than what they'd known with Eileen. Gabriel was no longer a carpenter. He simply could not be. He cleaned septic tanks instead. With Liam's help. Just as, when he'd built for others houses that sang, Liam had been there, too.

Liam wanted to help his father. Needed to. For it was Liam not Gabriel who remembered from estate to estate and season to season where the tanks were buried and how deep to dig.

From the start Liam helped with the digging, and when he was tall enough to do so, and clothed in hip boots and oilskins, he climbed with Gabriel into the tanks.

Father and son did their septic-tank cleaning only when Liam could be there to help. On weekends. In summer. After school.

Gabriel insisted that Liam attend school. Still. Even though their shared dream of his becoming an architect shimmered no more.

Liam was ridiculed at school. The loner who spent his every spare moment wading through sewage. But as Liam Pierce Rourke became ever more a man, and far faster than his classmates, he became infinitely intriguing to the girls— all the more so when his dark green eyes greeted their giggling stares with glittering intensity and unconcealed disdain.

Neither the proprietor of the cleaning company nor the owners of the septic tanks objected to the atypical hours the Rourkes worked. Father and son were unobtrusive, efficient, thorough.

Quiet.

Until those days in June. There was singing then, a wondrous duet, a capella magic beneath the Rocky Mountain sky.

Liam sang. And Gabriel sang. As did the cotton-candy clouds, and the butterflies and the roses, and the dump truck Gabriel drove.

Even the septic tanks sang. Here was a tenor. And here a baritone. And here, bellowing through its baffles, a basso profundo, its booming voice—once cleaned—pure and deep and clear.

The tanks sang. The world sang. And Liam's heart was singing too. Again. At last.

Gabriel and Liam cleaned septic tanks until two that Saturday afternoon. Then . . .

"Let's take the rest of the day off," Gabriel suggested.

"All right," Liam agreed. "Da?"

"Yes, Liam?"

"We both know what today is."

"That we do, my Liam. It's her birthday."

Her death day.

"Why don't we get cleaned up, all scrubbed and new, and dressed up, too. We'll make the dinner she was planning for us, and the cake we were planning for her. She'd want that, I think. Don't you?"

"Yes. I do." And it's time, Liam thought. It's time.

"Liam?"

"Yes?"

"I love you."

"I love you, too."

"You must sing, my Liam. You must *always* sing."

"I will. *We* will. And together, Da, we'll build houses that sing."

Liam showered first in the upstairs bathroom that he and Gabriel shared. Then, scrubbed fresh and neatly dressed, he went to the kitchen to begin the shopping list. The same items she'd bought that day. And from the same grocery.

Yes, my men! Eileen's emerald eyes had sparkled bright. You *will* bake my birthday cake. But I'd best buy the ingredients, don't you think? And supervise, just a little, when the time for making and baking comes?

When the doorbell rang at 3:52 it was Liam who answered it.

Gabriel was upstairs. Dressing. Liam had heard the shower, that song of raindrops, become silent, then the new music, his father's footfalls, singing heartbeats, overhead.

Liam opened the door to a quartet of elegance: two impeccably dressed couples backlit by the azure sky.

They were lost, Liam decided. This safe but far from glamorous neighborhood definitely wasn't *them*. They'd probably been en route to a wedding and taken a wrong turn. Many wrong turns.

Unless . . . the younger woman's pink-silk ensemble elegantly clothed, but did not conceal, her pregnancy. She looked in no distress, in fact was smiling. Glowing.

Still, with some urgency, Liam asked, "May I help you?"

"We may be a little early," she replied. "None of us was really sure what 'shortly before four' actually meant. I'm Valerie, and this is my husband Thomas, and"—she touched her stomach—"this is Melissa, assuming she's a she, and if she's not, well, the dialogue continues. We have time, three months, and the point is that she or he exists *as I do* because of your father, whom I cannot wait to truly meet. I was only ten when it happened and that day was such a blur, thankfully so, and—"

"Why are you here?"

"Your father asked us to be," Edward answered. "*Me* to be. But Lilah and Val and Thomas insisted on coming, too. They wanted to meet you. And of course your mother."

But Eileen Pierce Rourke had died.

Been killed.

On this date three years ago.

Shortly before four.

"*No.*"

Liam was halfway up the stairs when the gunshot thundered overhead.

*G*abriel Rourke had been suicidal in the way the genuinely suicidal are: calm, methodical, determined, clear . . . at least possessing a clarity which to his anguished mind made perfect sense.

Gabriel needed to be with Eileen. He had needed such reunion since the day she had died.

But Gabriel had survived for his son, loving Liam, caring for Liam, until the time came when his boy was old enough to go on without him—when, Gabriel's altered thinking assured him, Liam would be *fine* without him.

Such time had come sooner than Gabriel had imagined it would.

And as for the violence of Gabriel's death? It was methodically planned to match, to mirror, the violence that had befallen his beloved Eileen.

The coroner had strongly urged the bereaved husband not to view his dead wife's face. Not all of it and most certainly not in person. He would provide Gabriel with a photograph. Did.

Had Gabriel been content with that glossy print, his lasting image would have been of the half of her lovely face that was lovely still, her remaining emerald eye intact beneath her red-lashed lids, her lips curved in her familiar smile.

She'd been smiling when she died, envisioning the birthday evening that lay ahead even as she'd waited for the pedestrian cross light to signal green. Ever cautious, she'd probably even looked for stray cars before stepping off the curb.

But the speeding vehicle, its drunken driver at the wheel, had come from behind.

The eggs for the birthday cake her men would bake splattered on pavement so heated by the summer sun that in the aftermath they cooked, poached, burned.

And, in the aftermath, the left half of Eileen's face, all of it, was gone.

Gabriel's self-inflicted wound looked astonishingly like

Eileen's. But on the opposite side. When they met again, his desperate mind reasoned, and their faces touched, they would be one. Again. Forever.

Gabriel had wanted that. Planned it.

But he hadn't planned for Liam to see what had become of him, his half face with its half smile, and his vocal cords, tattered strings, that would sing no more.

Gabriel was certain that Edward would not permit his Liam to see, that Valerie's father would comprehend at once the favor Gabriel was asking and would grant it even as the echoes of the gun blast ricocheted in the air.

Edward did comprehend. At once. And that it was a significant request after all.

Save my son, Edward Prescott. Save his life. As I saved your little girl's.

Edward tried to prevent Liam from seeing his slain father. And Edward's physician son-in-law Thomas tried as well.

But Liam was Gabriel's son. He *had* to see. As Gabriel had needed to see Eileen, and hold her and cradle her and kiss *both* sides of her face.

Liam needed to do the same. He held his father's bloodied corpse, rocking him, whispering to him, kissing him, screaming at him . . . and refusing, for a very long time, to be pried away . . . even as the part of Liam Pierce Rourke that was so much already a man, with protective male instincts—primal, fierce, and sure—insisted, as did Thomas and Edward, that neither Valerie nor Lilah glimpse the carnage at all.

ONE

"elp."

Pierce heard the smile in the familiar voice and smiled in reply. "*Help*, Val? Don't tell me the mother-of-the-bride is getting cold feet."

"I think that's the bailiwick of the bride herself. Or the groom. Neither of whom, by the by, is showing even the slightest jitter. *Au contraire*. My destiny, apparently, is total emotional collapse scheduled to coincide, I'm told, with the precise instant that Melissa and Thomas begin their father-daughter march down the aisle. However, since that monumental instant is, let's see, thirty-seven hours, eleven minutes, and twelve seconds away—but who's counting?— I'm fine, utterly calm, an absolute *rock*. And my feet, as

21

it so happens, are really rather toasty. Which brings us back to *help*."

"Of course it does," Pierce asserted amiably. Val being Val would eventually make the not-so-obvious link between help and toasty feet eminently reasonable and crystal-clear.

Val being Val. Meaning distracted, and distractable? Hardly. The woman who'd just glanced at the nearest time-piece and calculated in a flash the hours, minutes, and seconds until the first note of the "Wedding March" would sound was focused. Always.

True, Val sometimes meandered. Her words did. But there was both method and message in her meanderings. Despite her easy flow of words, Valerie Prescott Evanson was more listener than talker. She merely created with the gentle flow a milieu in which others, especially those who needed it most, felt comfortable enough to speak.

It was a lazy river, that milieu she created. Leisurely. Welcoming. Come join the ride, her flowing words encouraged. Drift with me, meander with me. Speak, and I will listen. We'll float together wherever you want to go.

Valerie could also be quite direct. She'd been both with him—direct and meandering—during his first summer at Holly Hills.

Any room in the mansion could have been his. Even the one already decorated for the grandbaby to be. But he'd chosen to live in the remote cottage, vacant since Edward was a boy, and which bore a striking resemblance to the house in which Liam, Gabriel, and Eileen had lived.

Liam's new family undoubtedly realized the similarity,

and worried about it. *Him*. They were good people, Liam knew. Nice, gentle, compassionate, kind.

He sensed their helplessness. Their fear for him. But he didn't care, *couldn't*. His despair consumed him.

He wanted to be alone. And despite their worries, they permitted him to be. Edward, Lilah, and Thomas did.

But not Val. She became his shadow, close, constant, and not always silent. Even though he was silent. Until a sunny day five weeks after Gabriel's death.

He lashed out then. Suddenly. Explosively.

If she hadn't been *chattering* on his doorstep, hadn't being rambling *on and on* about her baby's name, he would have realized sooner why they'd come, what his father was planning, and would have raced upstairs in time.

His cruel outburst rocked them both. He'd hurt her. Wounded her. Frightened her.

But she did not run away.

She stood before him, trembling but determined, and Valerie Prescott Evanson, lady that she was, whispered what she must. "I'm *so sorry*."

He trembled, too. And whispered. Too. What he must. The truth. "It wasn't your fault. He was going to kill himself that day no matter what."

"But if you'd been able to *get* to him."

"No. Nothing and no one could have stopped him."

"Do you really believe that, Liam?"

"Yeah, Val. I really do. Don't call me Liam, though. Okay?"

"Okay." She waited, waited, waited. Finally, softly, "What should I call you?"

"My middle name. Pierce." Pierce not Liam, for Liam was love, *had* been. And now? *Liam* screamed, wept, pierced. *Pierce* did not. "All right?"

"Yes. All right. Pierce."

"And tell the others?"

"I will."

He was Pierce from then on, and she was his shadow still, more silent than chattering, intrepid yet wary, even though he didn't seem to mind, she thought, he really *didn't*, that she was there.

And when in early August it was Pierce who spoke, soliciting her words, perhaps missing them—"I feel like there's something you want to tell me, Val"—she answered with a message that meandered not at all.

"I'm *not* going to let you kill yourself."

"What?"

"I know how much you want to be with him, Pierce. With *them*. And that you miss them both as desperately as your father missed your mother. But that *isn't* what they want for you."

"I know."

"You do?"

"Sure. My father could have very easily taken me with him."

"No, he *couldn't*!"

"He sure as hell could have. He simply chose not to. Didn't want to."

It was the simple, bitter truth.

And it was rejected outright by Val. "Don't you know *anything*, L. Pierce Rourke? When one man saves another

24

man's daughter, and the hero later has a son, said son is responsible for that daughter for as long as she lives. It sounds backwards, I know. The *opposite* of what you'd expect. But that's the way all these ancient proverbs are."

"Val."

"It is. *Really.* Pick an ancient proverb, any ancient proverb. You'll see. They *never* make much sense." She met skeptical but attentive eyes. Intense eyes. And she saw for the first time the glint of emerald in the dark green depths. It was an inheritance from Eileen, this glitter, a dancing flame within the darker fire, a moonbeam at midnight in a forsaken forest. "Oh, all *right*! It's not an ancient proverb, just a pathetic truth. I've always wanted a little brother. I mean *always*, ever since I realized such creatures suitable for bossing existed. I'm spoiled rotten, haven't you noticed? I always get what I want."

She wasn't spoiled, Pierce knew. She was a trouper, fearless and fierce. And determined to have a little brother? Maybe. Val was at least determined to make certain the thirteen-year-old orphan survived.

Eating, she observed, would be an excellent start. And since words did not suffice—her little brother was choosing starvation still—she was compelled to show him by example.

Val gained more weight than she should have during what remained of her third trimester. And she must have been quite miserable tromping beside him in the summer heat. He'd been compelled to roam that summer, as if in pursuit of all that had been lost.

They roamed across the vast acreage of Holly Hills, their

combined shadow becoming ever larger as they wandered. Ever more bizarre.

Pierce grew taller that summer, lankier as he grew but did not eat, and his long black hair grew longer still, and lush and wild, even as Val, the shorter, rounder aspect of their single silhouette, grew ever more, ever more pregnant.

Maybe there was a proverb. The saved daughter rescues her rescuer's son and becomes his sister, his *sister*, after all.

It would be a while before "my sister" was spoken aloud by Pierce. Quite a while. But that's what she was in his heart by late September, when Melissa was born. Pierce couldn't say the words. Not then. Not yet.

But his gift to the new mother was eloquent, his own baby cradle, handmade by Gabriel, crafted with love from wood that sang.

Baby Melissa slept in the singing cradle as Pierce— Liam—had. And Melissa rocked in it. Her uncle Pierce rocked her.

Baby Melissa, who in thirty-seven hours and change would begin her bride's walk down the aisle.

"Val? Define help."

"Well, are you frantically busy?"

"Not busy at all."

"Really? I thought you might be engaged in a little heavy-duty glowering at this morning's *Post*, last evening's *News*, or quite possibly both? *Not* that a front-page above-the-fold story about you should come as the slightest surprise. Ever. And especially not now."

"Given that I'm the one who sent the construction crew home indefinitely."

"Given that, yes. But also given that it's Valentine's weekend *and summer*, weather-wise, as well. The editors needed to pull out all the stops to persuade the good citizens of Denver to brake their Rollerblades—and put romance on hold—long enough to buy a paper. What better enticement than that terrific photo they have of you along with an update on Carillon Square? You did happen to give them a little legitimate news." The tease but not the fondness vanished from her voice. "Is there really a problem with the project?"

"There really is."

"With the buildings?"

"No. They're okay."

"Better than okay, Pierce, from what can be seen from the street. 'Fabulous' springs to mind."

"Thanks. Let's just say they all work. The Commons, by contrast, does not."

"Oh, well, *that*."

That, the Commons, was the point, in the view of most, of the entire Carillon project, an open-air park framed by a four-story complex of restaurants, boutiques, and condominium homes.

Denver was a city of parks. Already. Was there truly a need, some had wondered, for another? Yes, the various public officials had ultimately concurred, because a park designed by Pierce Rourke would be, well, a masterpiece. By the master Pierce.

"How *not* right does it feel? Never mind. I know you

don't know the answer to that." Val also knew the several ways the not-rightness might be measured. In cost: thousands, hundreds of thousands, millions. In time: days, weeks, months. In torment for the architect: vast. Without measure. "Have council members or other investors been calling?"

"Not yet."

"Good. Why should they? They *know* you'll figure it out. It's just a matter of getting in touch with your inner feng shui or whatever it is."

Pierce knew what *it* was. But Val didn't. He'd told no one, even her, about his gift. He'd even believed for a while it had died with Gabriel.

But it hadn't died, merely slumbered, for a while. Years.

The buildings of Carillon Square sang, as buildings should, sweet and true and clear. But the Commons was worse than silent. It gasped, suffocating, drowning, beneath the vibrant songs of rainbowed glass.

Should he have known in advance the problem that lay ahead? Could he have known? Sure. If his gift enabled him to hear music from blueprints.

"You'll figure it out," Val repeated. "You just need a little more time to mull, stew, problem-solve. Which, as I recall, you've said can be accomplished anywhere. In fact, if I'm not mistaken, you've said that a change of venue sometimes helps the creative process."

"You're not mistaken. It definitely does. Are you about to change my venue, Val?"

"I am, assuming it's possible to do so between about

twelve-forty-five—I'm including transit time—and half past three?"

"It's entirely possible. I'm all yours."

"*Great*. Thanks. Because the *girls*, which is to say the bride, bridesmaids, mothers, and grandmothers, are having such fun being pampered at Chez Jacques that we're thinking we'll do lunch, Caesar salads, right here. Well, not *right* here. I'm in solitary at the moment, wrapped in seaweed."

"Hence your toasty feet."

"Hence my toasty feet."

"But your cell phone is with you."

"Always."

"And you're having fun." *Always.*

"Loads of it. Too much to think of leaving anytime soon. And the *guys* except for Thomas, who's seeing patients, talk about your father-of-the-bride *denial*, are golfing. Why not? It's summer! In any event, I need help with the little one. She needs to be picked up."

The little one. Val's daughter Callie. Who was nine.

"She's had enough luxuriating for one day?"

"She would have had, I can assure you, had she been here in the first place. But she opted out up-front in favor of school."

"That surprises me." It wasn't that Callie didn't like school. She did. But she idolized her big sister.

"It surprised us all once we tumbled to it, which we didn't right away. Callie wasn't going to say a word. But you know her. Even a trivial worry is like a massive cloud blocking the sun. It was Melissa who got her to admit the conflict and who convinced her she shouldn't feel the slightest guilt, she wasn't letting anyone down, and that languishing at a spa was, until one was quite a bit older, a total bore. Ha! I'm loving it. But Callie wouldn't have. Not today anyway. Not on book-club day."

"Book-club day? That's new."

"*Very* new and at present only for Callie's class. It was Callie's idea, Miss Finch claims, and Callie naturally says it was *all* Miss Finch."

"Miss Finch."

"The librarian."

"Also new."

"As of December 1. You remember from your stint on the board the issue of Mrs. Broaddrick's retirement? Whether she really *wanted* to or not?"

"We decided 'or not.' Even though she'd been talking about it for years."

" 'Or not' was what the current board decided, too. And we certainly weren't going to push, not even a gentle nudge, because we were all so worried about what she'd do with the free time. Then Miss Finch appeared. Out of the blue. She'd never worked in a school, she admitted, but every time she drove past the building—which she'd been doing frequently since her arrival from Boston a few weeks before—it beckoned to her."

"So she just dropped by one day and became the new librarian?"

"Not quite that dramatic, but pretty close. She *is* a librarian. And the timing was perfect. Mrs. Broaddrick's recently widowed sister in La Jolla wanted her to move there *stat*, to get settled in before a Christmastime Hawaiian cruise."

"*Stat* may fly in hospitals," Pierce observed. "But it's not the way of things, of *anything*, at Hazel Traphagen's School for Girls. I speak from experience."

"I know. The board is *The Board* no matter who's on it. But you would have been impressed, Pierce. Miss Finch wasn't hired on the spot, of course. She had to jump through all the usual hoops, and then some. But the entire vetting process was accomplished in record time. Her credentials are impeccable, and she's also a computer whiz, which is a nice plus, since the girls are so computer-savvy these days, and Mrs. Broaddrick *really* wasn't."

"Miss Finch sounds very new millennium."

"Yes. But she's traditional as well. Quite passionate about good old-fashioned reading from good old-fashioned books. And the girls *adore* her."

"Do the parents adore her, too?"

"They, we, appreciate her. *A lot*. I'm not sure any of us truly sees what the girls see."

"Which is?"

"Mary Poppins meets Socrates."

"Ah. Of course. What does that mean?"

"Well, she gets the girls to think à la Socrates. She encourages and respects every thought they express. It's the girls, not Miss Finch, who make the book-club selections from week to week."

"And à la Mary Poppins?"

"She's *magical* to the girls. All of them. Every girl in every class. Even the sixth-graders despite their imminent graduation to the terrible teens. Too bad the school's oft-proposed expansion to grades seven through twelve is eons if ever away."

"Callie will never be a terrible teen."

"Who'd've thought Melissa would be? But she *was* as you recall. Thank goodness for you and Thomas and Dad."

Pierce did recall. Achingly. It had nearly killed Val when her beloved Melissa, her sweet little firstborn, had needed to assert her identity as a woman-to-be, distinct from Val. Virtually overnight the bubbling "Mom! Guess whats?" had become disapproving "Oh, *Mothers.*"

"Our only value as *you* recall, Valerie, was our gender. Which makes me wonder if Miss Finch would really fare better than any other woman at that difficult time."

"Maybe not. Anyway, we'll never—oh, hi! No, it's fine, come on in. It seems, Pierce, that I've *marinated* long enough."

"So Callie's expecting to be picked up when?"

"One-fifteen. She's doing lunch after book club. Then if you could just drive her home? I should be back no later than three."

"You and the rest of the marinated and manicured entourage?"

"No. Just me. The others are going to swing by the golf course to be sure the guys are on track to make the rehearsal and assorted festivities on time."

"I'd be happy to stay with Callie beyond three."

"Thanks. But *my* guy, my neurologist in denial, is reading EMIs, not golfing."

TWO

*F*ounded in 1906, Hazel Traphagen's School for Girls had been before its girls-school incarnation a gold miner's home. The prospector had struck it rich, staggeringly so. But greedy for even more, he took risks and lost everything. During his golden days, however, he'd built one of Denver's finest mansions.

No structural alterations had been necessary in the transformation from home to school, although the infrastructure had been upgraded apace with technology. From electrical wiring to double-paned glass, Hazel Traphagen's was state-of-the-art.

Depending on their age, the girls walked or cantered, in a ladylike way, up a central staircase that was pure *Gone With the Wind*. The banistered stairway divided halfway up its grand ascent, which is where the students divided, too. The upper classes, grades four through six, veered left, while grades one through three, the scamperers, galloped right.

Hazel Traphagen's signature color, fragrance, and flower had been violet. The original school uniform had, accordingly, been a fashionable ensemble of white middy blouses and violet bloomers.

The girls wore white blouses still, a modern cut, with violet jumpers or skirts. And in a decision debated by three successive boards, knee-high stockings in lilac, marigold, or pink were also approved.

Traphagen when correctly pronounced was Traa*pay*gun. A student was therefore a "Peggy," as Hazel Traphagen herself had been.

Lilah Prescott had been a Peggy. She still was. All alumnae were. Val, Melissa, and now Callie had happily followed suit.

Val had recruited Pierce to serve on the board at the beginning of Callie's first year. "You'll be an honorary Peggy, Pierce, and we'll all be *so* proud!"

He'd served faithfully for the prescribed two-year term and could, this academic year, have chosen to re-up. But he hadn't, nor had anyone pushed. All of Denver knew what was on his architectural plate.

But he *should* have re-upped, Pierce thought as he drove into the familiar circular drive. He could mull, stew, problem-solve anywhere. Even, he dared not tell Val, *especially* at board meetings.

He hadn't even heard about Miss Finch, or book club.

34

Maybe that was why the clever Val, his bossy big sister, had sent him on today's mission—to remind him gently, although he was feeling distinctly jarred, what he was missing.

Well, he thought, I'm back.

No matter that Carillon Commons didn't sing, might never sing, and that his next project was consequently indefinitely delayed.

He might even volunteer to appear, *re*appear, when it was once again Callie's turn for "show-and-tell." Not that there was much new to tell, that could be told . . . which didn't mean the wily nine-year-olds, so forthright in their innocence, wouldn't ask.

The second-graders had certainly been incisive last May. At age eight.

He'd gone to their spacious second-floor classroom, a lavish bedroom once. The eighteen pupils, up from twelve in Val's day, were assembled in a circle, which Pierce joined; part of it, not inside it.

Show-and-tell had begun as always with an introduction by the girl who'd arranged for the special guest.

Callie had written her introduction and faxed it to Pierce to make certain he approved. Then she memorized it, Val told him, and rehearsed and rehearsed and rehearsed.

When the moment came Callie clutched a typed copy in her hands just in case. And when she spoke? The sunny child, so much like her mother, abandoned entirely her carefully prepared script.

"This is my uncle Pierce! He's an architect, as you *all* know. Well, maybe Janie doesn't, since she's only been in

Denver for a month. Except you *are* from Chicago, Janie, and there *is* a Wind Chimes there. Anyway, something everyone may *not* know is that Uncle Pierce used to be a lawyer. A *prosecutor*. Like when it's the People of Colorado against some criminal? Uncle Pierce was for us, the people, and he won *every single case*! He would have *kept* winning. But he decided to become an architect instead. Which is even *more* lucky for us, the people, including . . . you live in Cherry Hills Ranch, don't you, Mara? Well, guess what? Uncle Pierce designed your house. Yes, *really*. And yours, too, Laurel. It's great, isn't it? And totally *different* from Mara's? None of the houses are the same, even though Uncle Pierce designed *every one*. All the houses, the entire neighborhood, won a very important architecture award."

Callie's uncle Pierce designed condominiums, too, including the Canterbury just a mile away and Mountain View Place downtown. And speaking of downtown, her uncle also designed every Wind Chimes Hotel and Towers, the eight in the continental U.S., and the ones in Paris, London, Monte Carlo, and Quebec.

Residents of the Towers, home to luxury condominiums on the top floors and to offices below, enjoyed all the amenities of the adjoining five-star hotel. And many Towers residents, Pierce included, experienced the ease of commuting from home to work by elevator. Or by stairs.

The Maui Wind Chimes was in the planning stage. Tropical elegance in the Hawaiian Isles. And as soon as the Pine Meadow Conservatory was finished—it wasn't *yet*, Callie said, because it wasn't *quite* right—construction would begin on Carillon Square. There were many *other*

Pierce Rourke creations, past and future, *so many,* and they were all really *amazing,* too.

"But his *tour de force,*" she asserted, "is the Island."

Callie paused. Briefly. To catch her breath even as her rosy cheeks beamed ever more brightly at the grown-up phrase used and pronounced correctly. *Tour de force* was, Pierce felt quite sure, a recent acquisition from Val.

"That's what it's called," Callie continued. "The Island. And that's *all* it's called. When you say 'the Island' in Denver, Janie, everybody knows what you mean. They also know that if you're going to the Island, you're going to a *wedding.*"

The Island had never even *had* another name, Callie explained. No one had really even known it existed, unless they'd just happened to be flying by, and the prospect of building on it *definitely* didn't exist until her uncle Pierce.

"Half of it's pure rock, you see. Like the moon. *White* rock, though. Like snow. And the other half, where flowers and trees are everywhere, is home to families, *neighborhoods,* of birds. Disturbing their homes is something Uncle Pierce would *never* do."

Pierce had built atop the barren moonscape. Atop, and under. Elevators from the entirely subterranean—sublunar—parking garage opened into the building above. Or, if a wedding guest so chose, the ascent to the moon gardens could be accomplished by stair.

And how did one get from land to island? By a tunnel, as invisible as the garage, beneath the lake.

Pierce placed lush gardens amid the snowy drifts of stone, and fountains sang in the shimmering ponds, and the building itself was wedding-cake white and adorned year-round with wisteria, a bounty of lavender blossoms and emerald vines fashioned entirely from glass.

White-marble bridges arched over the Island's myriad ponds, and the garden paths were heated in winter, the *rock* was heated, so wedding guests could wander, could marvel, without fear of mishaps on ice.

"And there are tiny white lights *everywhere*, like little twinkling stars, and I could go on and on! But"—Callie sparkled like those heavenly lights—"I think I might have already gone over my five minutes."

The introduction of the special guest was, except for the girl whose turn it was to introduce, a small part of show-and-tell. More important was the question-and-answer session that followed.

Pierce's appearance had been scheduled weeks in advance. There would therefore be, Val forewarned, significant parental input, maternal input, in many of the questions the girls would ask. Inquiring minds, after all, wanted to know. And these eight-year-old girls, eight-year-old daughters, were at an age when their mothers were still their best and most influential friends.

Janie, the newest Peggy, went first. Her question was not surprising and probably all hers, focused as her mother was on settling her family into their new home.

What had made him want to be a lawyer? Janie wondered.

Well, Pierce thought but did not say, his mother had been killed by a drunk with numerous convictions for DUI, a man who long before that life-shattering June should have been safely sequestered in jail. And a similar fate for a similar reason might have befallen Callie's mother—and Callie might never have existed at all—had not his own father intervened.

An abiding belief in law and order, Pierce replied. And in justice. And, he told the lovely innocents, in making the world safe.

But why had he quit? Especially when he was so good?

Because revenge, he thought but did not say, was empty, aching, cold—even when served on a winning streak . . . and because some criminals, so many, were far more pathetic than evil, human beings turned monstrous because they'd never known love. Which didn't mean they shouldn't be locked up. They should be. *Had to be.*

But did Pierce find satisfaction in denying freedom to such creatures, innocents once, innocent once, who'd never had a chance? No. None at all. Sadness, yes. Sorrow, constantly.

And what of his pledge to make the world safe? By seeing that the nightmares of society, however pathetic they might be, were safely, securely, put away? Well, there was merit, too, in making the world beautiful. Wasn't there? In trying to? By creating places of song, of singing, of dreams?

It was simply time, Pierce answered, for him to move on. And, he suggested to the bright little girls with such boundless potential, there was no rule that you had to have just one career, the same career, your entire life.

Besides, Liam Pierce Rourke heard himself confessing,

becoming an architect had been his dream even before becoming a lawyer had.

Laurel *loved* her house, she told him. She was *so glad*
he'd designed it. And she really, *really* loved her room.
Mara echoed the sentiment with comparable enthusiasm.

Then it was a girl named Robyn's turn. She began with
a gushing testimonial, too. She'd been to a wedding on
the Island, and it was *so beautiful*. Was it true he'd met
with wedding specialists before starting to build? So that
everything on the Island was as wedding-friendly as it could
possibly be?

Absolutely true, Pierce replied. He'd had sessions not
unlike today's show-and-tell, except that it was he who'd
been asking the questions—of coordinators and caterers
and florists and clergy. And of newlyweds, too, brides and
grooms, and their families, all of whom had offered excellent advice.

Was it terribly expensive to buy the Island? a girl named
Bobbie asked in a rush and with a furtive glance at their
teacher, Mrs. Jones.

Ladies did not, Bobbie knew—they all knew—pose specific questions about money. Such queries were impolite,
both in show-and-tell and in life.

But this query, undoubtedly prompted by a curious parent, wasn't specific, exactly. A precise dollar amount hadn't
been requested, nor even if the price tag had been in the
mid-to-upper seven figures, or the low-to-middle eight.

Mrs. Jones made a silent ruling. Bobbie was teetering at
the edge of propriety. But she'd not stepped over the line.

Besides, Mrs. Jones was interested in the reply. In Pierce's every reply.

No, Pierce answered. Not terribly. Especially since the purchase price had included not only the island but its cliff-wreathed lake and forests beyond.

He'd bought it, he thought, *for a song*. He'd had no choice. Even from the air, the snowy rocks had sung to him.

But it was probably pretty expensive to *build* there, Bobbie persevered. On the rocks and under them, and under the lake as well.

Yes. Pierce smiled. It was.

But worth it?

I think so, he answered, even as Callie and a chorus exclaimed *yes*!

Was the Island really nonsmoking?

Yes. It really was.

Because he believed that people shouldn't smoke?

That was his belief, Pierce admitted. The evidence was overwhelming that smoking caused harm. The Island's nosmoking policy was not, however, a one-man crusade against cigarettes. The consideration was practical, not presumptuous.

Fire?

Yes. Although, he reassured, with the sprinkling system he'd installed, the tiniest flame would be quickly doused. It was the smoke, he said, that concerned him. The smokiness. The building was furnished like a welcoming home, with plush carpets, billowy sofas, embroidered lace drapes.

"*Plus*," Callie added, "Uncle Pierce cares about bird

lungs, especially *baby*-bird lungs. He cares about drinking, too. Drinking and driving. It's *okay* to drink, if you're old enough, but not to drive."

It was *his* island, after all, Pierce's niece explained. He could make what rules he liked. He only made *good* ones, though. Of course! Ones that made the weddings happy *for everyone* from beginning to end.

Designated drivers, who were off-duty cops, attended every Island wedding where alcohol was served. It was a requirement, which was welcomed, appreciated, over time, when it became understood that the cops, dressed like guests themselves and blending right in, were there not to police, not to judge, but to protect.

"Isn't that *great*?"

Callie's query evoked enthusiastic nods, even from a girl who'd been frowning in anticipation of the question it was her turn to ask.

Did it hurt his feelings that he'd never been named Denver's most eligible bachelor? The honor bestowed by *Mile High* magazine in its December/January issue every year? Did he feel *slighted* that he'd been overlooked?

Not slighted at all, Pierce reassured the young faces suddenly troubled *for him*, Callie's wonderful uncle so terribly wronged.

*D*elighted, he amended silently. Besides, a silent musing still, he wasn't truly eligible. Yes, he believed in marriage. Very much and with reverence. Witness the venue he'd created for the celebration of such vows.

And it wasn't that thirty-six-year-old Liam Pierce Rourke didn't enjoy the company of the opposite sex. He did.

Most definitely. As the women of Denver enjoyed, most definitely, *him*.

But Pierce became restless in relationships. *Became* restless? No. He started that way.

What about glass sculptress Giselle Trouveau? an earnest inquisitor queried once Pierce's assurance had been sufficiently absorbed.

The Giselle question, fully anticipated by Val, was a logical follow-up to the bachelor one. Indeed, it was accompanied by a flurry of nods—inquiring mothers had wanted to know—and with a gasp but silence from Mrs. Jones, and with pure exasperation from Pierce Rourke's emotive niece.

Callie's freckled arms flew into the air, her typewritten introduction fluttering like a dove, and she embarked on what Pierce assumed to be her personal rendition of what she'd heard Val say on the subject many times.

"There's *nothing romantic* between Uncle Pierce and Miss Trouveau! Yes, she's *really* beautiful and *really* talented. And *of course* Uncle Pierce likes her. And it was really great, *perfect*, that they were already working together, because of the Wind Chimes, when Uncle Pierce bought the Island. Miss Trouveau is American, even though her name is French, but she's lived in Venice. Italy. The Island reminded her *right away* of Venice. Even from the air. It was all the water, probably, even though it's canals in Venice and ponds here. Uncle Pierce agreed. He built bridges just like the ones in Venice, and found the *exact* same lampposts, too. There are no *gondolas*, however. That would be *troppo*, which means 'too much' in Italian. There's *wiste-*

ria, though, on the Island, as in Venice. There's barely any room for *real* gardens in Venice. But thanks to wisteria, the Venetian gardens are *on* the walls. And thanks to Miss Trouveau, there's wisteria, made of glass, on the Island. It's incredible, the blossoms look *so* real, and, like in Venice, it's *everywhere*."

The Island was, Callie asserted, Giselle Trouveau's *tour de force. Too.* But the glass artist's relationship with the architect was, she reiterated, *strictly* professional.

Which, Pierce mused as his niece expounded, was entirely true.

What he knew about Giselle, and what she knew about him, was only what was necessary, pertinent, to their admittedly spectacular collaboration.

Giselle didn't know that Pierce's buildings sang, *had* to, and he had no idea what compelled her to create shapes from fire. He knew only that her vision was as clear as his, and that she was as passionate about her art as was he.

"Besides," Callie informed her classmates, as if it were the definitive icing on the strictly professional cake, "she lives in Carmel, California, not here."

So you *aren't* going to marry her? a persistent or perhaps frequent-flying second-grader asked.

"No!" Callie's arms flew anew as a smiling Pierce concurred, "No. I'm not. And more significantly, she's not going to marry me. You ladies would all make excellent attorneys."

That had brought to a close last May's show-and-tell. A

week later Pierce received nineteen handwritten thank-you notes. Mrs. Jones penned one, too.

And if he returned to the circle this May? Would Carillon Square be stalled permanently because Denver's premier architect had been unable this time to find a way out?

It was just as well, Pierce decided as he pressed the doorbell at the front entrance of the school, that an encore appearance wasn't in the works.

The mansion door swung open before the bell finished its cheery chime. All outside doors were locked, Pierce knew, when school was in session. Hazel Traphagen's had been that way, that safe, since Valerie Elizabeth Prescott's near abduction thirty-six years before.

The sixty-four-year-old woman who greeted Pierce wasn't imposing in the least. But, he knew, she was armed with knowledge. Security cameras had tracked him from the moment he'd driven through the massive stone pillars. And should the need ever arise, panic buttons, both portable and installed, were in abundance throughout the school.

"Mr. Rourke!"

"Hello, Mrs. Holt."

Mr. Rourke. Mrs. Holt. It was all so Charlotte Brontë. Proper. Traditional. The respectful formality of a time gone by. The school's adults, including its parents, were as impeccably trained, impeccably Peggy, as the girls.

"Are you here to collect your niece?"

"I am."

"She's *so* excited about the wedding and absolutely *thrilled* that Melissa has chosen her as maid of honor."

Pierce smiled. Despite some rather difficult teenage years, the always loved Melissa had not surprisingly blossomed into a lovely young woman. Nine was simply too old, Melissa had told her bedazzled little sister, too grown-up to be a flower girl. Besides, Melissa explained, she *needed* Callie right beside her holding the gold wedding band she would be giving to Doug.

Pierce's smile held even as a deep frown furrowed Mrs. Holt's brow, the consequence apparently of whatever she was reading in Callie's administrative file.

"Oh, dear."

"Valerie"—Mrs. Evanson—"didn't call?"

"Yes. She did. Two days ago. She said she'd be picking Callie up at one-fifteen."

"I'm early. And in no hurry. Or is there another problem?"

"Not a *problem*, really. Just a little red tape. You're not actually listed, you see, as someone who's authorized to take her out of school. Why would you be? We all *know* that Callie's your niece, and even if you were coming to pick up one of the other girls we'd know it was *safe*, that she'd be safe with you. *Of course.* The trouble is I'm not really permitted to make exceptions. Even ones as easy as this. Although I suppose . . ."

"Mrs. Holt? Let's not bend any rules. There must be a protocol for dealing with such situations."

"Well, yes. There is. Mrs. Fairchild. Unfortunately she's not here just now."

"There's probably someone who's second-in-command?"

But there wasn't, Pierce decided. Mrs. Fairchild, a Peggy

herself, had been headmistress for forty-seven years, with an attendance record, he gathered, that was quite unblemished until today.

Pierce was determined not to get annoyed. Indeed the notion of a little successful problem-solving had enormous appeal.

"There must be a teacher, Mrs. Holt, who could approve?"

Mrs. Holt's frown became a smile. "Yes. Of course. Miss Finch."

Pierce concealed his surprise. In this school where tradition was everything, Mrs. Holt's choice of the newcomer librarian seemed remarkable.

But Pierce wasn't about to argue with a minor crisis so promptly resolved. And it would be interesting to meet the improbable blend of Mary Poppins and Socrates.

Maybe even fun.

"Great," he said. "I imagine she's in the dining room?"

"No. She's not." Mrs. Holt embellished further as they crossed the marble foyer to the library, a journey that took them beneath a chandelier of violets that was a gift to the school from Giselle. "Book club's a bit fatiguing for her, I think. She needs a little rest in her office before the afternoon's computer classes begin."

Miss Finch was becoming more interesting, although perhaps less fun. Pierce had imagined someone young, more big sister than mother—or *grand*mother. How else to explain Val's conviction that Hazel Traphagen's new librarian could survive as a role model even when the girls reached the difficult teens?

How else? As the Peggy of all Peggys, Pierce supposed. A spinster of a certain age and from a different era, complete with seamed hose and sensible shoes, who even now was sipping from fine china a spot of chamomile tea.

"That's odd," Mrs. Holt murmured as they encountered in the library a circle reminiscent of the one he'd joined for show-and-tell. "The girls didn't return the chairs to the computer cubicles before leaving for lunch. And unlike every other book-club day, they finished early not late."

"I'd be happy to return them."

"No," Mrs. Holt replied. "If the chairs were left like this, it's because that's how Miss Finch *wanted* them to be."

THREE

*P*ierce added "strict" to his descriptors of Miss Finch. And as Mrs. Holt tapped lightly on the librarian's office door he added "very" to that.

Very strict.

And very Charlotte Brontë. A lifelong keeper of books who could detect even the faintest whisper at a hundred paces.

Paces?

Mrs. Holt's light tap was too tentative, Pierce thought. Scarcely audible. Even for the exquisite hearing of the venerable—

Miss Finch. Who was thirty at most, and slender and tall. She stood ramrod straight without the slightest teeter despite the height of her far-from-sensible heels. Her navy blue suit was woolen, as was the cream-colored turtleneck she wore. An outfit for the dead of winter on this summer-in-February day.

Pierce couldn't see her face. She'd been looking down even as she'd opened the door. Expecting her visitor, he decided, to be a little girl.

Mrs. Holt wasn't tall to begin with, and she wore sensible if modern shoes. Nikes. Miss Finch towered and gazed downward still. Pierce saw only her hair, the lustrous sable subdued primly yet bountifully at the nape of her neck.

Prim. Proper. Rigid. Frigid.

Very.

Except that Pierce had a surprising image of her kneeling had her visitor been that little girl, a graceful curtsy despite the constraints of her tailored navy skirt so that she might gaze directly at the young and possibly troubled face.

Miss Finch's voice when she spoke was music.

"Yes, Mrs. Holt?"

"I'm sorry to bother you, but Mrs. Fairchild had that doctor's—"

"Yes. How may I be of help?"

"Well, Mr. Rourke is here to collect Callie as Mrs. Evanson had previously arranged. The only problem, and it's *scarcely* a problem, is that Mr. Rourke's name isn't in Callie's file as someone to whom she can be released. I thought you might be willing to assume the responsibility of making an exception to the rule?"

"Oh. I see. Yes. I . . . certainly." The librarian's ice-white fingers retrieved Callie's file from Mrs. Holt's rosy ones. "Thank you, Mrs. Holt. I'll handle it from here."

Mrs. Holt, thus politely, musically, summarily dismissed, disappeared. And Miss Finch looked for the first time at him.

And Pierce saw for the first time her face. Her bright blue eyes, her skin of snow.

It was an aristocratic face. Serious, intelligent, and registering as it gazed at him? Nothing. Not a flicker of recognition, and most assuredly not a smile.

"Mr. Rourke? Please come in."

She opened the door wide and left it that way.

Pierce entered an office that was as neat and tidy as she. But unlike the woman with snow-white skin and clothed in layers of wool, the office was warm. Hot. Its thermostat set for the deadliest of winters.

There was color on her desk, a kaleidoscope of crimson, a bouquet of joy. And adoration. The lacy red Valentines were neat and tidy. Too.

And so carefully arranged, Pierce realized. So *thoughtfully.*

No matter its size, each card was fully visible, uneclipsed by any other, equally welcomed, equally cherished—as were the sensitivities of each and every card-giving girl.

Good for you, Miss Finch.

Pierce's thought came with a smile for the pale woman who'd moved to the other side of her mahogany desk. She was seated across the assembly of Valentines and a little confused, Pierce thought, by his smile. Its gentleness for her.

Confused. But focused. Gesturing for him to sit as well, she asked, "May I have your full name, Mr. Rourke?"

"Liam Pierce Rourke."

"And Rourke is spelled . . . actually if you have a driver's license I could just get the necessary information from that."

"Sure." Pierce retrieved his wallet, removed the license, and handed it to the librarian and computer whiz with a passion, according to Val, for good old-fashioned reading from good old-fashioned books.

The Passion of Miss Finch. How Charlotte Brontë could one get? Surely good old-fashioned reading, not to mention Boston-proper librarianship, included the occasional glance at the news? The front page for example, either online or in print of last evening's *Rocky Mountain News* or this morning's *Denver Post*?

And there had been at checkstands everywhere and for a solid two months the December/January issue of *Mile High* magazine, its eligible bachelor issue featuring his name and face on every cover. The *in*eligible bachelor slighted no more.

And delighted not at all.

Miss Finch really could not have missed seeing the magazine.

Not if she shopped.

Not if she ate.

Was the austere librarian playing with him? Had she not only seen the cover but read the story within? The chronicle of architectural feats so dazzling when finally finished that the good citizens of Denver willingly forgave even the most inexplicable delays—the imperfections that were invisible to them but monumental, or so he claimed, to him?

Invisible. Like the emperor's new clothes.

Miss Finch might have reasonably concluded that such delays—coupled with the invisible imperfections—signaled an ego so inflated it created faux crisis to garner the attention it so desperately craved.

More fuel for such egotism, if more was needed, was provided by candid comments from various women he had known. Dated. Slept with.

The man who was uncompromising in his commitment to quality in the buildings he designed was similarly uncompromising when it came to his personal life. The quality was spectacular, the physical intimacy truly dazzling. But, his lovers knew because he told them from the outset, the relationship was not destined to last. For Pierce was above all uncompromising when it came to his commitment to remain emotionally uncommitted.

Personally uninvolved.

Miss Finch, accomplished reader that she was, could have decided that unlike the rest of Denver, Pierce's women included, she wasn't fooled by the pompous emperor. She'd expose his naked arrogance once and for all by pretending she didn't have a clue who he was. Not his face, not his name, not his fame.

And when the supremely arrogant architect responded with outrage and pique? Her point would be elegantly made.

Pierce would have been quite happy if the Boston blue blood truly hadn't the foggiest notion who he was.

And maybe she didn't.

Maybe she hurt *far too much* to play. The thought, the truth, came as Pierce watched her methodical transfer of his driver's license data to Callie's administrative file.

Her head hurt. Terribly. And had been hurting terribly, the lilac beneath her eyes suggested, throughout the night.

She hadn't slept. Her head ached. And she was cold.

Yet she was approaching the responsibility Mrs. Holt had placed on her delicate shoulders with the utmost care. Just as, Pierce mused, she would have knelt before a worried schoolgirl no matter the discomfort it caused.

She was running on gossamer fumes. The *per*fume, Pierce realized, of violets.

"Miss Finch?"

She looked up. Slowly. Testament to the pain evoked by the simple movement of her head.

"Yes?"

"Let me make this as easy as possible. I'm Callie's uncle. Valerie Evanson's brother. As you may know there's a wedding in the works." Pierce was stopped by the glow in her bright blue eyes. Fondness amid her pain. "Callie's mentioned this?"

"She has." The smile on her ashen face shimmered. Then faded.

"Val, who's involved with nuptial festivities, asked me to pick Callie up. Since I'm not listed as being authorized, I think you should call Val to confirm. I'd give you her cell phone number"—*so that you don't have to move yet again your pounding head*—"but it's probably more appropriate for you to get it from the file."

"I got the impression from Mrs. Holt that I should know who you are and that such checking shouldn't be necessary. But I don't know. I *would*, I'm sure, if I watched TV, or had been reading the papers, or if I'd seen the Super Bowl?"

"I'm an architect. From time to time and far more often than I'd like, someone decides that what I'm up to is news. Even if you had recognized me, there'd be no reason not to confirm what I've told you. Val would want you to, *will* want you to. Callie's safety is paramount to us all."

Thus encouraged, and referring as he'd suggested to the number in Callie's file, she reached for the phone that had been displaced to the edge of her desk by Valentines.

The call was answered right away.

"Mrs. Evanson? This is—yes, that's right. Yes, he is. No, his name isn't . . . there's no need to apologize. I'm sorry to have bothered you but . . . yes, it is school policy. No, one can't be too careful. Thank you. I will. Good-bye." She returned the receiver to its cradle, then looked at Pierce. "Your sister said we could add your name to Callie's list. If you like."

"I would like that. But what I'd like most at this moment, and more far importantly, is for you to tell me how long your head has been hurting."

"My . . . ?"

"Head. It's aching, isn't it? Pounding."

"Yes."

"And you're quite cold, aren't you? Chilled?"

"Yes, but . . ."

"And I even have the feeling that it's uncomfortable for you to move your neck."

"It is. A little. But . . ."

"You could have meningitis." Pierce said it softly. Carefully. Not wanting to alarm. But she wasn't alarmed, merely surprised. By the decisiveness of his pronouncement? Or the gentleness of his concern? Pierce addressed the first. "No, I'm not a doctor. But my brother-in-law is, which means my very bright sister has in essence gone through medical school as well—and, like him, is learning still. Val's particularly diligent about learning, and sharing with her family, the illnesses of children, many of which also affect the adults in their world. Meningitis is classic."

"I don't have meningitis."

She said it wistfully, Pierce thought. Wishingly. As if as terrifying as a diagnosis of meningitis might be, it was preferable to the one she had. Inflammation of the meninges was treatable after all, *curable* in most instances when caught in time.

And the diagnosis that was hers? This woman of violets and Valentines who was so aching, so cold? So *pale*.

Her mane of sable, if knotted, was luxuriant, as if untouched, never touched, by chemotherapy. As if even the most aggressive medical interventions wouldn't help. Couldn't help.

"I'm sorry," he whispered. "I shouldn't have pried."

"It's all right!"

"Are you?"

"Yes. Truly. I am. It's nothing, really. A nuisance. An annoyance. That's all."

An annoyance that caused coldness, sleeplessness, a head pounding with pain? That wasn't "nothing, really" in Pierce's book.

So he pried a little more.

"A nuisance that's been fully worked up?"

Surprise shimmered anew. Astonishment this time. And, this time, it was his gentleness—and his gentle persistence—that seemed to truly amaze.

"Yes. Thank you."

"By someone good? My aforementioned brother-in-law is a neurologist. One of the best."

"Yes. I know. I've seen Dr. Evanson. There were certain . . . things I felt the school should know before they hired me."

She'd jumped through all the usual hoops, Val had said, *and then some*. Including a consultation with Thomas? Apparently, yes.

Why?

Pierce would have gently persisted further, had not a freckled ray of sunshine beamed brightly, politely, from the open doorway.

"Hi," she said. "May I come in?"

"Of course, Callie," the librarian welcomed.

And Pierce, standing, greeted, "Hey, kiddo."

"Hey, kiddo!"

"Your mom asked me to pick you up."

"And you weren't too busy?"

"For you, Callie Evanson? Never." *Never again.*

She looked older, as she did every time he saw her, no matter how brief the interval had been. Her hairstyle was particularly grown-up on this day, her strawberry blond curls knotted, it was supposed to be a knot, at the nape of her neck.

À la Mary Poppins.

Socrates.

The intriguing Miss Finch.

"And you met Miss Finch! Mrs. Holt told me you weren't authorized, even though you *should* be."

"And now I am."

"Good! Are you feeling better, Miss Finch?"

"Much better, Callie." She looked at Pierce. Wonderingly. And, as if he were responsible for the *much better* that she felt, she said to him, "Thank you."

"Thank you, Miss Finch," he replied very softly. "For taking such good care of my niece." Then to the niece who seemed almost as bewildered by his words as was Miss Finch, Pierce said, "So, Mademoiselle Callie, are you ready to hit the road?"

"Totally ready. Happy Valentine's Day, Miss Finch!"

"Thank you, Callie. Happy Valentine's Day to you, too."

"Happy *wedding*, you mean."

"Yes. That's right. Happy wedding." Her voice was a whisper as delicate as a bride's lacy gown as she embellished to Callie, "Be careful."

FOUR

"*I* can't believe it!" Callie's pronouncement came beneath the glass violets of Giselle Trouveau's shimmering chandelier.

Neither can I, Pierce thought.

Be careful, Miss Finch had warned Callie. Be careful of what? *Him?*

Couldn't the librarian tell just by looking at him that he was not a monster? Could not possibly be?

No, apparently, she could not. And Pierce's reaction to the inability of her bright blue eyes to see? Fury. *Fury.* Swift, molten, and surprising for him. Rare.

And irrational, he knew. Unreasonable. A reaction as rare for him, as surprising, as fury.

Pierce imposed the stern voice of reason.

Of reality.

One needn't have been a deputy DA to know that so-ciopaths came in all stripes: rich, poor, uncle, brother, ar-chitect, attorney. In-depth media coverage of criminals and their crimes made such knowledge commonplace. And given the widely publicized *charm* that often accompanied sociopathy, the diagnosis could not, as any informed per-son knew, be excluded during a brief conversation over Valentines.

Still, it infuriated him.

It felt, he realized, like betrayal . . . except that betrayal was what one felt when there'd been love . . . when, for example, your father had chosen death over life, more life, with you.

"Can't believe what, Callie?"

"That I left my knapsack in the dining room! How dis-combobulated can I be? It must be those wedding jitters that nobody except me seems to have. Can I go get it, Uncle Pierce? Do you have time?"

"I've got all day, Callie-Callie. And you know what? There's something I need to discuss with Miss Finch. It might even take a while. So find your knapsack *slowly* and we'll meet back here."

*P*ierce had no intention of knocking softly on the li-brarian's office door. Of knocking at all.

He was reaching for the knob as the door flew open.

They collided, she collided with him, for she was moving swiftly, determinedly, distractedly.

She would have fallen had Pierce not caught her. He felt through the woolen sleeves of her navy blue suit the thinness, the tautness, the ice beneath.

Balance restored, she stepped out of his embrace. But not away. Even when she saw the glittering—and unconcealed—fury. It only encouraged the words she'd already planned.

"I'm so *sorry*. There's no excuse for what I said. *None*. It had to do with *me*, an experience I had, and *nothing* whatever to do with Callie. Or you. Is she terribly upset?"

"She's not upset at all. Callie's pretty accustomed to hearing such admonitions from the adults in her world."

"But *you're* upset. Why wouldn't you be, after being so concerned about my headache? After *helping* me. It."

"You think my concern helped?"

"I . . . yes. It did. And now I've repaid your kindness by—"

"Doing nothing wrong. I was upset," Pierce conceded more easily than he would have imagined he could. "But not anymore. I remain concerned, however, about you. Your headache's still better, I think, but you're freezing cold."

"Freezing cold," she echoed. "And out of control."

"Because of what you said to Callie?"

"*Yes*."

"That's caring, Miss . . . hell, do you have a first name?"

"I'm Ana." Her head tilted thoughtfully, and without

pain, and when she spoke it was a soft confession. "Anastasia."

Anastasia, Pierce mused. The lost princess. "Talk to me, Anastasia."

"About?"

Anything. Everything. You. "Why you have headaches, why you're so cold. Not that it's any of my business."

"But it *is* your business. Because of Callie. Mrs. Fairchild was supposed to have sent your brother-in-law's assessment to all the girls' families. I hope she did. I *wanted* her to."

"Then she undoubtedly did. To parents, I would guess, not uncles. I do know my sister has only the most glowing raves about you. Rave upon rave. Which, we can safely assume, means Thomas had no misgivings at all. Did he?"

"No."

But *she* had misgivings, Pierce thought. Grave misgivings about herself. "I'd go with Thomas's evaluation, Anastasia. He really is the best at what he does."

"He's also very nice."

"Not at the expense of the truth."

The truth. Which was what? Pierce wondered. Not a secret, apparently. Anastasia had prompted the evaluation herself. There were certain *things*, she'd said, she felt the school should know. After which she'd authorized Thomas and Mrs. Fairchild to disclose the results.

"Thomas found an answer to the headaches and coldness?"

"An explanation anyway."

"One that you'd be willing to share with me? Feel free

to say no"—Pierce smiled—"concerned though I might be."

"I'd like to tell you."

"But you're frowning."

"Isn't Callie waiting for you?"

"Not yet. She's on what's supposed to be a leisurely search for her knapsack."

"Okay. Well, I guess it would be best to close the door. Although it's awfully hot in here, isn't it? For you?"

Too hot for him. Too cold for her.

"It's fine," Pierce said as he closed the door. "I'm fine."

When they were seated as they'd been before, across an expanse of mahogany and Valentines, Anastasia began.

"Last July, at a wedding reception in Boston, I drank some lemonade laced with drugs."

"Drugs? Plural?"

"Yes. Rohypnol and GHB."

As with "sociopathy" in a media world, one needn't have been a prosecutor to be familiar with both Rohypnol— roofies—and gammahydroxybutyrate. GHB.

"Date-rape drugs."

His voice was very soft.

His eyes were very green.

Too soft. So green.

She was lost for a moment, as lost, as lovely, as her name.

"Anastasia?"

"Date-rape drugs. Yes. But that *wasn't* what happened. Not to anyone. It wasn't even the intent. The culprits were seven-year-old boys who'd overheard an older brother telling a friend about Rohypnol. When you gave it to a girl, he bragged, she'd do whatever you wanted and remember nothing after. That sounded like hypnosis to the boys. And fun. Like a stage-hypnotist act they'd seen. A cousin's upcoming wedding reception, complete with video cameras to record the antics, seemed an ideal opportunity to give the drug a try. So they raided the brother's stash."

"And put both Rohypnol and GHB in your lemonade."

"Yes. Although they didn't know it was mine. Didn't know me. I selected the tainted glass myself. The only lemonade glass, as it turns out, they'd tampered with. Their primary target was the vodka punch, into which they sprinkled, poured, only GHB. The first guests to sample it became promptly and violently ill. Even as they were being rushed to the nearest hospital to have their stomachs pumped, the boys were confessing all."

"You weren't one of those guests?"

"No. I'd wandered with my lemonade to the garden. When the whirling hit, I fell to my knees, it was impossible to stand, and crawled beneath a massive rhododendron. I slept there, was unconscious there, until morning. When I came to my head was pounding and I was shivering despite an overnight temperature near ninety. I've had the headaches and the coldness off and on ever since."

"I like the sound of 'off.'"

"Thank you. So do I. And both the headaches and coldness *are* off from time to time. For days sometimes, and once for almost a week."

"Does Thomas think it's unusual to have the headaches still?"

"No. And he, like the physicians I saw before leaving Boston, believes the coldness can be explained by some thermoregulatory disruption caused by the combination of drugs we know I received, or by whatever other drugs might have been tossed in."

"Did they find evidence of other drugs?"

"Not in my blood. But there was homemade LSD in the apartment of the chemistry major who'd concocted the GHB. It would have been undetectable, even if I'd ingested significant amounts, by the time the blood studies were done."

"Are you having flashbacks?"

"No." She hesitated only a heartbeat. "Just flash forwards. *One* flash forward. A dream. Very lovely, and very real. It's *here*, the place in my dream, even though the dream began in Boston and I'd never been to Denver before."

"A dream déjà vu, especially a lovely one, doesn't sound so bad."

"No. Not bad at all. And not really worrisome, I suppose, as unusual—for me—as such prescience is. And not worrisome at all compared to the sequelae that explain why I didn't know who you are."

If she'd been reading the papers, she'd told him, or watching the news, or maybe the Super Bowl? "My feeling about the Super Bowl," Pierce said, "is that there's very little point in watching unless the Broncs—or Patriots?—are playing. And since the news these days can be pretty grim, avoiding it from time to time makes perfect sense."

"But I watch *no* television. Before leaving Boston, I gave my TV away. And there's no part of the paper, either, that I read. I've shut out the world, you see. The *real* world. Shut it out since last July."

Pierce did see. Her worry. Her despair. And Pierce felt the sharp ache of remembrance, his own—those months during which Gabriel Rourke had shut out all but his lethal, meticulous, determined plans.

"Because?" he asked.

And waited. Patiently. Restlessly.

"I've needed silence. Uncluttered. Undistracted. Absolute."

"Because?" he asked again. Softly.

"So I can concentrate on listening. For what I don't know. Voices, maybe?"

"Are you hearing voices?"

"Only yours." Her smile was faint. Beautiful. Fleeting. "I have this feeling that if I listen long enough and hard enough, I'll hear something, *something*, I'm supposed to hear. Crazy, huh?"

Crazy. So that was it. She feared that the drugs she'd been given, especially an undetected dose of LSD, had induced, were *trying* to induce, a psychosis of sorts.

"Not crazy, Anastasia. Courageous." Far more courageous, Pierce reflected, than the grieving son who for a very long time following Gabriel's death had chosen *not* to listen to silence, had resisted it mightily, even though he'd known the glorious sounds he would hear. Anastasia's silence was mysterious, a vast unknown, an uncharted terrain created by the same alchemy that had brought her a lovely dream, throbbing headaches, and bitter cold. But still she listened. Still she explored. She was a pioneer, this princess. "I'd be willing to bet Thomas doesn't think you're crazy."

"You'd win that bet." *For now.*

"Anastasia?"

"Yes?"

"What else?"

"Nothing." Everything. She felt so safe at this moment with him. *Safe.* How crazy was that? "Nothing. Thank you for listening."

"Thank you for telling me."

She wasn't dismissing him, Pierce decided. Even though, quite clearly, the revelations had come to an end. Before all had been revealed? Yes, he thought, was thinking, even as a knock sounded on her door.

Was this why the revelations had ended? Because she truly could hear the faintest whisper, or softest footfall, at a hundred paces?

"That's probably Callie," he said.

"No. That's not her knock. It belongs to a first-grader named Helen." Anastasia glanced at her watch. "Who's right on time. She's been having trouble with the computer. We arranged to go over a few things before the rest of her class arrives." She looked from her desk of Valentines to him. "Would you open the door, just a little, and tell her it will be another minute or so?"

"Sure."

Pierce stood, turned, and looked down even as he opened the door. Looked down as Anastasia had, then knelt as she would have to better converse with the very young face.

Pierce wasn't convinced this very young face would converse with him, no matter how gently prompted. But before he could offer such prompting her eyes widened and the realization gushed.

"You're Callie's uncle!"

"That's right, I am. Hi. And you are?"

"Helen. My sister Laurel's in Callie's class, and we live in a house you designed. We *love* it!"

"I'm glad."

"And we love the Wind Chimes, too! And Carillon Square, even though it's not quite finished yet! And we're all going to Melissa's wedding on the *Island*! You really designed it? It's really *yours*?"

"Yes, and yes. I had quite a bit of help, though, very good advice when it came to the design."

"I can't *wait* to see it!"

"Well. I hope you like it. And speaking of waiting, Helen, Miss Finch asked me to tell you that she hasn't forgotten your appointment, but wonders if you'd mind waiting another minute or two?"

"I don't mind! I could put the chairs back."

"That would be *lovely*, Helen," Anastasia's musical voice from behind him affirmed. "Thank you."

As Helen twirled and dashed, Pierce turned to Anastasia, who was staring at him.

"I really should have known who you are. I know your buildings. Marvel at them. I just didn't realize they were yours."

"They belong to whoever enjoys them." *They're yours, Anastasia. If they sing, Anastasia, to you.*

She was an architect herself, this woman who arranged Valentines so that young hearts would flourish. Except that now her desk was barren.

She was building, however, designing anew. *About* to. The crimson bricks for her new creation lay in a neat stack on her mahogany desk.

"Those are Valentines from Helen's class, aren't they? And the previous batch was from Callie's?"

"I have eighteen from every class. One from every girl. I'd like to display all of them all the time, but I simply don't have room."

"This way's better. More special."

But not yet under construction, and needing to be. Helen was waiting. And perhaps by now Callie was waiting, too.

Time to say good-bye, and all Pierce wanted was more hello.

Did she?

"I wonder if a wedding followed by a reception without a drop of tainted lemonade would appeal to you? I just happen to be going to such an event tomorrow night. Would you like to come to Melissa's wedding with me, Anastasia? Will you?" Pierce had his answer. A surprised yet glowing yes. *Yes.* Hello. More hello. "Why don't I pick you up at—"

"No."

"No?"

"Thank you very much for inviting me. But I can't go."

She said it wistfully, wishingly. As when she'd told him

69

she didn't have meningitis. Did she want, wishingly, to say yes? But was she compelled, wistfully, to say no?

For what reason, Anastasia? What aren't you telling me?

Pierce would have his answers. Sometime. Another time. During their next hello. Or their next. Or their next.

"Okay." He smiled. "Happy Valentine's Day, Anastasia."

"Happy Valentine's Day . . . Liam."

FIVE

"I'm so glad you met Miss Finch!" Callie enthused at the onset of their drive to Holly Hills. "And that *she* met *you*. Isn't she nice?"

"Very nice."

"I'm glad she's feeling better."

"So am I."

"I hope *her* wedding is as perfect as Melissa's is going to be."

Liam—Liam, Liam—Pierce Rourke did not in response to Callie's remark drive off the road. Not this man whose mother had been killed by a drunken driver out of control.

Pierce kept his car traveling straight and true even as his thoughts veered, his emotions skidded, and his plans

71

came to a screeching halt. He'd already been thinking about when he'd call her. How soon. *Soon.*

"Miss Finch is getting married?"

"Well, *yes.* I mean she will, won't she? *Someday?*"

"Sure she will." *Of course she will.*

"I hope it's okay that I went to school instead of to Chez Jacques."

Pierce focused his remarkably restive thoughts away from Anastasia's someday nuptials to the wedding scheduled for tomorrow night. "I just happen to know, and this is according to your mom, that it was *more* than okay. Especially since to the best of my knowledge seaweed's never really been your thing."

"Seaweed?"

"Your mom was wrapped in it when we spoke. Hermetically sealed. Except for her phone." Pierce smiled, and his niece giggled. "It was much better, Callie, for you to have been at school."

Pierce kept his eyes on the road. But his peripheral vision was excellent, and his passenger's young face, her entire being, was so expressive he could almost see her thinking. Could almost hear the whir.

"If I *hadn't* been," Callie began as her whirring thoughts found voice, "then Mom wouldn't have had to call you to pick me up."

"True."

"And you wouldn't have met Miss Finch."

"Also true."

"So it *was* good I was there."

Oh yes.

"Plus, if I'd missed book club, I wouldn't have learned about Grace. Uncle Pierce?"

"Callie."

"When's Mom getting home?"

"By three."

"Oh."

"But I'll be there, Callie, if there's something you need. Which I gather there is?"

"Well, yes. Maybe. I mean, you are *authorized* now. You could read the article first, while I was dressing for the rehearsal. Then if you said it was okay, I could read it, too."

"The article?"

"In this week's *People* magazine." Callie touched the knapsack at her feet. "I have a copy. Erin, whose turn it was to choose for next week's book club, gave all of us copies."

"You need permission to read the article?"

"Miss Finch made us promise."

"Is that usual?"

"No. But I think she was worried that the subject matter was PG-13. For violence. For *sadness*. And also, I guess, because the story was real. *True*."

"Real violence. True sadness. I find myself agreeing with Miss Finch."

"The thing is, Uncle Pierce, we all already know about the violence and the sadness. The way book club works is that whoever's doing the choosing tells us about it first. And even though the story was true, Erin introduced it the way we always do, like a fairy tale, beginning with 'once upon a time.' There's violence in fairy tales. Quite a bit. And until the end there's usually quite a bit of sadness, too. Miss Finch had no idea the story was real until Erin started taking the copies of *People* out of her bookbag. It wasn't her *fault*. She's from Boston, not Denver. There's no way she'd know there's really a town in Colorado named Loganville."

A town in Colorado named Loganville. A girl called Grace. And sadness, and violence, and . . . Pierce, from Denver, knew.

How he knew.

"Was Erin's story, the *People* story, about Grace Alysia Quinn?"

"*Yes!* You know about her, Uncle Pierce? And that horrible fire on that Christmas Eve?"

"Yes, Callie. I do." As did—had then—all of Denver, all of Colorado, and, he imagined, the worried citizenry of all bordering states.

It had been twenty-three years since the Yuletide inferno in Loganville. But Pierce remembered it blazingly still. The tragedy had occurred during his first Christmas at Holly Hills, just six months after Gabriel's death, and it had changed Pierce's life again. Profoundly. Irrevocably.

For the better.

Grace had changed it. Grace Alysia Quinn. The five-year-old who'd died in flames with her mother, Mary Beth.

Generous, joyful, gracious, kind. The words defined both mother and child. Mary Beth and Grace had welcomed a teenage stranger into their home, and they'd been murdered, both of them, for their kindness.

It had been Christmas dawn before the charred skeleton of the house on Bluebird Lane had been cool enough for Loganville's chief of police to go inside and discover murder. By that time the teen killer could have easily hitchhiked to Denver, and beyond.

But he'd be in Denver, Pierce had decided. The killer. And he, Pierce, would find him, and would avenge, when he did, the searing slaughter.

Pierce had roamed the wintry streets possessed, obsessed, pacing, prowling, and fueled by a rage that had been smoldering since Gabriel's death. Since, perhaps, Eileen's.

A tiny spark had flamed last summer. The outburst at Val that had stunned them both.

But it had been such a trivial spark, Pierce realized as he prowled for the Loganville killer and felt the true potential of the embers within.

Did the family who'd welcomed him so graciously into their Holly Hills home have the slightest insight into the tinderbox he truly was? Had they worried even before the Loganville horror what their own tormented teen stranger might do?

And did the Loganville carnage provide an all-too-vivid blueprint for what in their heart of hearts they surely feared: that Liam Pierce Rourke, whose father had chosen such violence in his own death, might choose violence for them all—might shatter Valerie's skull as Mary Beth's had been shattered, then condemn the others, baby Melissa included, to death in flames.

In terror.

Pierce knew terror intimately, had known it during those scant instants of excruciating clarity between comprehending what Gabriel was intending to do and the thunder of the gunshot overhead.

Scant instants. A forever loss.

Pierce had been a mature thirteen on that devastating day. He had known death, known loss, once before. And there'd been for Pierce a quartet of good people, wonderful people, willing to help, to comfort, to try.

But, Pierce wondered as he searched the shadows, what of the five-year-old innocent named Grace? What of *her* terror alone in her bedroom, trapped by a killer, and knowing her mother lay dying in the living room below?

He saw her in that bedroom, that little girl sanctuary of ruffles and lace, and he heard the flames, felt the fire, inhaled the smoke.

Grace Alysia Quinn's terror had been protracted. Minute upon minute. An eternity of knowing she was going to die. Of screaming for help. Of pleading for mercy.

There'd been no help, no mercy, for the terrified little girl. No quartet of kindness standing close by.

Pierce knew as he prowled the icy streets that he could vanquish the Loganville murderer with his bare hands. His naked fury. Could. Would. So ravenous was he for the kill, so hungry, so hungering for revenge.

But as he prowled, he prayed. For Grace. And as he prowled, as he prayed, Liam Pierce Rourke was changed by Grace . . . by grace.

He returned to Holly Hills with empty hands and open heart. And did he see disappointment on the kind faces that for all these months had concealed every morsel of their fear? Sorrow that he hadn't simply wandered away?

No. Pierce saw only relief that he was home. Pierce thanked them all. Reassured them all. He wasn't homicidal, he told them. They had nothing to fear. They didn't look, these kind people, as if they'd ever been fearful of him. But they looked worried now, so worried until he said the rest, that he wasn't suicidal, either.

There was more relief then, shimmering and pure.

Relief. Home.

Pierce set goals for himself after that Christmas of Grace. He'd become an attorney, he decided. He'd make the world safe.

It was a noble purpose, an honorable pursuit. But, for him, empty in the long run. Aching and sad.

Still, it was that pursuit that kept him alive, encouraging him to survive, to flourish, until he was ready—his heart was ready—to become the architect he'd been born to be.

The Passion of Liam Rourke. He owed it to Grace Alysia Quinn. In her death she'd given him life. Purpose. Passion.

In her death. Twenty-three years ago.

Pierce had no doubt the little girl could reach, still, from her grave, could bestow more gifts, more purpose, more grace. Still.

But hadn't there been enough contemporary tragedy for Callie and her classmates? Ample, abundant, present-day horror?

JonBenet.

Littleton.

The trial in Denver of Oklahoma City bombing suspect Timothy McVeigh.

The lessons had been learned. Surely. The world was not always a safe and loving place.

This week's *People*, Callie had said. Even that made no sense. What recent news there'd been, and there most definitely had been some, had come and gone six months ago. In August. When the real Loganville killer had been revealed.

He was not, after all, the runaway teen. Yes, the teen had fled. And yes, it had been a flight of guilt. But it had been a shepherd's guilt, not a murderer's. A shepherd consumed with remorse for failing to protect his flock.

The true murderer, the authentic monster, had been . . .

"Troy Logan," Callie was saying as if cued by Pierce's thoughts. "Logan as in *Logan*ville. He was in love with Grace's mom, but she wasn't in love with him, and it made him so mad that he killed her. Isn't that awful, Uncle Pierce?"

"Yes, Callie. It is. But what I don't understand, and I imagine this is Miss Finch's thinking, too, is what's the point in your reading about such sadness?"

"Because it isn't completely sad!"

Well, true. Troy Logan was dead. He'd been killed on the very verge of murdering yet again, and just moments after confessing all, gloating all, to his would-be victim.

Troy was dead. Grace could rest in peace. At last. Still . . .

"It's pretty sad, Callie."

"No, it's not! There's a happy ending. At least there can be. *Will* be. She's alive, Uncle Pierce! Grace Alysia Quinn is *alive*."

SIX

*C*allie showed Pierce the cover of *People* when they reached Holly Hills.

It was okay—permission-wise—for her to do so, since the cover had been revealed during book club. And she and her classmates had studied it even more, she confessed, during lunch.

"We didn't *open* the magazine though, since we'd promised Miss Finch we wouldn't. And the other stuff Erin told us during lunch was okay I think, I really do, because it was about the plans for finding Grace *now*, not more about what happened that night. Erin knows those plans because her aunt Dinah was Grace's *very best* friend."

It was Dinah, Callie explained, who provided the cover photograph of Grace. The portrait of happiness, a photo booth snapshot, had been taken just three days before the Christmas Eve blaze. It was so lucky, Callie added solemnly, that Grace and her very best friend had decided to pose for photos on that day, because every picture Mary Beth had ever taken of her daughter had burned to ash.

"Isn't she pretty, Uncle Pierce?"

"Very pretty."

The photograph of Grace, of cloudless innocence and boundless joy, was encircled by images of other key players in the drama. Old images, twenty-three years old, precisely as they'd looked to Grace when she'd seen them last.

Callie knew them all.

"This is Erin's aunt Dinah when she was five. She and Grace were in the photo booth together. You can even see, right here, a strand of Grace's hair. And this is Grace's mom. Mary Beth. She's so pretty, too. And this is Dinah's mom, and the town librarian Mrs. Bearce, and . . ."

Here was the teenage shepherd not killer in a summertime photograph taken at the lake; and here Grace's kindergarten teacher; and here the Quinn's nearest neighbors on Bluebird Lane, whose palomino Sunshine, pictured too, Grace had loved to visit, to feed, to pat.

Loganville's chief of police, who was police chief still, was pictured. As was Denver neurologist Dr. Howard Kline. Pierce knew Dr. Kline. As did Callie. The revered physician had been Thomas's mentor, then his colleague, as he was still. In his eighties, Howard Kline was teaching still, inspiring still, and respected always.

"Dr. Kline was involved?"

"Yes," Callie replied. "But I don't know *how*. It's in the article, though. Erin didn't tell us at lunch because of our promise."

"Maybe I should read the article."

"You want to?"

"I do. Okay?"

"Yes. *Okay*. I'll go upstairs and change. And Uncle Pierce? You don't have to give me permission if you don't want to. I can wait till Mom gets home."

In a moment she was off, scampering aloft, the final straw, Pierce noticed, for the knot at the nape of her neck. Callie made a promise before scampering, a vow both solemn and aglow.

"We're going to find you, Grace. Don't *worry*, we will."

Worry was Valerie Prescott Evanson's second reaction when, thirty seconds later, she found Pierce and *People* together in the living room.

Val's first reaction was a smile. "Hallelujah! My perennial Christmas quandary, what to give the brother who wants *nothing*, at last is solved. From here on, Pierce Rourke, I'm giving you a subscription to *People*. Or not," she added as she met his gaze. "What's up?"

"I was just about to start reading an article for next Friday's book club. It's an article, Val, about Grace Alysia Quinn."

"The girl who was murdered in Loganville?" Val asked as she set her purse, her car keys, and today's just-delivered mail on the coffee table between them. "I *do not* want Callie to know anything about that. I can't believe Miss Finch—"

"She didn't realize until most of the story had already been told that it was true."

"How could she *not*? Okay, admittedly the Christmas Eve fire might not have been big news in Boston, news in Boston at all, twenty-three years ago. And she would have been just a girl herself. But the story was definitely a national one last August. It's not every day a man of Troy Logan's prominence is revealed as a maniacal killer."

But it was in July, Pierce thought, that Anastasia had begun forsaking the news and listening to silence in the hope that she would hear *something*. "In any event, Val, there's new news. Grace is alive."

"What? How?"

"I don't know. I was about to find out. I gather from Callie that the answers are here." Pierce offered Callie's *People* to Val. "Be my guest."

"No, Pierce. Be mine." Valerie retrieved her own copy from the day's mail. "I *do* subscribe."

They read in silence, and at virtually the same pace, skimming what they already knew and reading with great care what they did not.

Grace had jumped from her second-floor window, a desperate leap from smoke to snow. She'd lain unconscious in a snowdrift overnight, kept warm, kept alive, by a blanket of ash.

It was Troy who'd spotted the golden hair amid the layer of soot. He would have murdered her then and there had not his fiancée Carolyn been with him.

Together, and secretively, Troy and Carolyn took the injured girl to Troy's Splendor Mountain home. Grace's miraculous survival was necessarily shared with Loganville's funeral-home owner, who pretended to receive and inter beside her parents the little girl's charred remains.

The secret was also shared necessarily with Dr. Howard Kline, whom Troy had called at his Denver home on Christmas morning. Troy had met the eminent neurologist at the various medical center fund-raisers he made a point of attending and donating to lavishly.

Secrecy was essential, Troy explained to his unwitting accomplices. The only way Grace would truly be safe was if her killer believed her dead.

And, Troy added ominously, he wasn't entirely convinced that the teen fugitive was the murderer at all. There were others in Loganville who might have caused Mary Beth harm. *One* other, Troy amended, without naming names.

It wasn't necessary for Troy to provide his suspect's name to Carolyn. She knew well the man who'd been spurned not once but twice by Mary Beth, and who'd reacted the first time with violence. Rawley Ramsey. Loganville's chief of police. The funeral-home owner also knew whom Troy meant, although he liked Rawley and doubted it could be true.

Dr. Kline didn't know, nor did he ask. His only concern was for his five-year-old patient.

Grace was stable enough upon awakening to remain right where she was. She needed neither neurosurgery nor an ICU. All she needed, in fact, was time. Which she had. Her life expectancy would be entirely normal, Dr. Kline forecast. As would she be in time.

Her muteness was emotional. Logical. A not-unexpected

consequence of the psychic trauma she'd suffered. The silence would reverse. She *would* speak again. And until then? With faint but decisive nods and shakes of her battered head, she responded to every question that was posed.

Could she hear? Yes. Did she understand all the words that were spoken? Yes.

Did she know her name? Where she lived? How old she was?

No. No. No.

Her amnesia, Dr. Kline felt quite certain, would be permanent. And it would be both retrograde—her entire life before the fire—*and* antegrade: the days, weeks, possibly months that followed.

Dr. Kline provided Troy with names of pediatric psychiatrists from whom, Troy subsequently claimed, he'd received referrals to the best inpatient psychiatric facilities for children in the world.

Which was where Mary Beth's amnesic daughter would go. Troy would take Grace there himself, he told Carolyn, without ever specifying where "there" was. And when the traumatized girl was speaking at last? And making new memories? It would be best—Troy said the psychiatric consultants advised—for her to be adopted by a loving family with no connection whatsoever to Loganville.

Grace would be physically safe that way, her very existence forever concealed from both the fugitive teen and Police Chief Ramsey.

She would be emotionally safe, safest, too, away from the town where she might be haunted, her subconscious might be, by phantom memories and invisible ghosts.

Troy and Grace left Splendor Mountain on the night of January 12. Troy returned one week later. Alone.

He'd "gotten rid of her," he'd gloated twenty-three years later. And cleverly, too. *So* cleverly that the "person or persons" to whom he'd given her were as clueless to her identity as was she.

But Grace was definitely alive, Troy asserted during those boastful moments before his own death. At least she *had* been when he'd seen her last. And there was really no reason to imagine she wouldn't be alive, living, still.

Troy's revelation had been greeted with hope, with joy, by the people who'd loved little Grace. They weren't her blood relatives. She had none left. But she had an entire town—and a teen shepherd turned trauma surgeon—that cared very much.

The search for Grace was private at first. And meticulous, thorough, complete. Loganville memories were searched, as were scrapbooks and photo albums; and every square inch of Troy's Splendor Mountain mansion, and his plane, his office, his car; and the papers of Troy Logan, both personal and professional, every remnant of the life of one of Colorado's wealthiest men.

And? Nothing. Not a lead. But the months of private investigation were far from a waste. They formed the rock-solid foundation for the public search that was commencing with this week's *People*, this very special Valentine to Grace.

Grace Alysia Quinn would be twenty-nine. The five-year-old had turned six two weeks after she'd supposedly perished in flames. It hadn't been a commemorated birthday,

Troy's widow, Carolyn, confessed. Nor even, she said, a remembered one.

The woman Grace had become might easily believe herself to be younger—or older—than her twenty-nine years. And what would she look like, that woman?

It was impossible to know, a distinguished panel of forensic pathologists concurred. Predicting the bone structure of the adult from the few surviving photographs of the very young girl was risky at best, fraught with uncertainty, as likely to be wrong as right.

No such artistic renditions, therefore, were offered.

Grace's eyes would, of course, be blue. And her hair, in all likelihood, would be blond. *Very* blond, as she'd been as a child and as both her parents had been as adults.

A photograph of Grace's critical-care nurse mother at age thirty appeared in *People*. Loganville Hospital also found in its archives a photograph of cardiologist Samuel Quinn, Grace's father, who'd died in a one-car accident—an accident, definitely—a week before his daughter's birth.

Grace at twenty-nine might resemble her mother, her father, a marriage of both. And although she might not perceive a resemblance, wouldn't be looking, wouldn't *know* to look, a colleague might, or a spouse, a lover, a friend.

And it was even possible that someone might remember seeing the golden-haired girl with the man who was Troy during that January week long ago. Assuming, that is, the sociopath hadn't disguised them both.

"Tell me this isn't hopeless," Val said. "Tell me this isn't a search for a golden needle in a meadow of haystacks. Many, many, many meadows."

"It's going to be tough," Pierce conceded. "Not that there won't be many, many, many needles—some golden, some not—volunteering to be found."

"Many, many, *many?*"

"I'm afraid so. And those are just the legitimate ones, the legions of blue-eyed blond-haired women hoping to be Grace, wanting to be, and believing absolutely that they *might* be. My prosecuting days gave me a fairly sobering insight into just how many lost little girls with lost little childhoods there really are."

"You never mentioned that."

"What would have been the point? In any case, there will be no shortage of legitimate candidates."

"And impostors, too."

"Impostors, too."

No mention had been made of the immense fortune awaiting Grace. There'd been no need to. The riches were as self-evident as the awaiting love.

A wrongful-death lawsuit against Troy's estate, which Grace had every right to file for his murder of her mother, would very likely yield a significant chunk of the killer's staggering wealth—assuming Troy's childless widow and unwitting accomplice didn't just bestow a fortune or two the moment Grace was found.

There would be impostors, fortune-seekers, many, many, many.

"And it's going to be difficult, isn't it, to discern the legitimate contenders from the false?" Val asked. "If parental DNA were available, that significant bit of data would most certainly have been disclosed. Don't you think?"

"Yes. I do."

Which meant, Val thought, that Mary Beth, charred beyond recognition, and Samuel, mangled from the car crash, had been interred as ash. Just as Pierce's own violently ravaged parents had been.

"So we're back to hopeless," she said softly. "Grace doesn't have the foggiest idea who she is, if she's even still alive, and there's no way to prove who she is in the event, by some miracle, she happens to appear, and now Callie and her classmates are emotionally involved. Don't get me wrong. I think Grace's loved ones should be searching for her. How could they not? If it were me, and no matter how long the odds, I'd move heaven and earth to find her."

"Which is what they're doing."

"It is, isn't it?"

Any lingering doubts about either the magnitude of the love or the vastness of the money behind the campaign to find Grace were laid to rest at the end of the article. The *People* Valentine was just the beginning. More articles would appear in the weeks and months to come, and both daytime and prime time television specials had been scheduled. The web site *www.findinggrace.com* featured hot links to every article ever written about the Loganville fire, more photos, and a bulletin board for those with information they wished to post.

The search was being coordinated by Chicago attorney Garek McIntyre, who with a small army of investigators would be following every lead. Both 888 and Chicago phone numbers were provided, as well as e-mail and e-fax.

"And they're doing it right, aren't they?" Val asked. "You had experience with searches and tip-lines when you worked with the DA."

"They're doing it very right, Val. Including triaging away from Loganville the operational center of the search. I'm quite sure that Rawley Ramsey wanted to set everything up in the police station there. To run the investigation himself. Given his reputation, he undoubtedly *could* have done it, and well. But placing someone in charge who's not emotionally invested—and who's geographically re-moved—is definitely wise."

"Have you ever heard of Garek McIntyre?"

"No."

"He certainly has good taste when it comes to where he works. And lives. Do you suppose he really wanted *People* to disclose that both his law office and private residence are in the Windy City's Wind Chimes Towers?"

"My guess would be yes. Given the care with which the investigation has been done, beginning with the initial pri-vate phase, I'd say Garek McIntyre leaves very little to chance. The come-one, come-all, around-the-clock invita-tion for information, even to his home, sends the clear message that any tip, however trivial it might seem, is more than welcome."

"It's not entirely an around-the-clock invitation. At least not a live and in-person one. I read that right, didn't I? That callers between 11 P.M. and 7 A.M. will be greeted by a tape recorder only?"

"You read it right. And that's advised, too. More proof that Mr. McIntyre knows his stuff. True, crank calls peak between midnight and dawn. But there are also those with potentially valuable information who prefer both the cover of darkness, even over the phone, and the anonymity of leaving a recorded message. Garek McIntyre knows what he's doing. I just hope he has enough help."

"You could help him. Former prosecutor that you are." Val's head tilted thoughtfully. Knowingly. "You've already decided to help."

"To offer at least. There may well be a disproportionate number of tips, and candidates, from the Denver area. Those that can't be vetted by phone will need face-to-face interviews."

"Which you'd be happy to do."

"Very happy." Happy. And objective? In this search for the girl who changed his life?

"Well, *good*. With you on the case, maybe there's hope after all. I still wish Callie didn't know a thing about it."

"But she does. I wonder if Anastasia could use some help."

Val arched an interested, sisterly eyebrow. "That would be Ana—Anastasia?—Finch?"

"Here's a news flash, Val. In the real world, men and women exchange first names on a fairly regular basis." First names. Given names. Parental gifts of love that changed over time. With tragedy. With circumstance. With the loss of dreams. But he was Liam again. Liam with her. And she was Anastasia, not Ana, with him. "Amazing but true."

"Ah." The eyebrow arched a little higher, a final punctuation before drifting down. "What did you mean she might need help?"

What he'd meant, of course, was that maybe he should offer to help her. Today. Right now.

Wishingly, and so willingly. Hello again, Anastasia. *Hello.*

But did Anastasia *need* his help? Hardly. Pierce knew what she'd tell her book-club girls, her sensitive senders of Valentines, when they worried about what would happen to Grace if she was never found. Hazel Traphagen's librarian would echo the reassurance offered by Loganville's librarian Mrs. Bearce, that Grace Alysia Quinn, who'd been so very loved, would remember that love, her heart would, and she'd be *just fine.*

"Pierce?"

"It was just a thought, Val. Which, as I think about it, was wrong."

SEVEN

"*H*ouston, we have a problem."

Pierce turned from a glass fountain sparkling in moonlight to wedding coordinator Frances Donahue. Frances had been among the many specialists he'd consulted, one so helpful he'd queried her a number of times.

Frances prided herself on glitch-free weddings. Pierce's aim had been to provide a beautiful—and functional—venue for same.

And, but, now? Despite her *Apollo 13* comment, Frances didn't appear terribly worried, as if the problem was not insurmountable, even though they were at T minus forty-five minutes and counting.

"A problem, Frances?"

"We've lost our wedding singer. Which is to say our wedding singer, the groom's mother's college roommate, has lost her voice. Laryngitis. So far she's squeaked the news only to me. I was on my way to discuss the options with Val when I spotted *you*, the bride's uncle, hence family. But likely to be totally calm about last-minute decision making. Not that Val wouldn't be. But laying any new issues on the mother-of-the-bride at this late stage is something I'd rather not do."

"Okay, Frances. Give me the options."

"Well, I see three. One, find a replacement. *Try* to. And get him or her here on time. Two, find a replacement and delay the ceremony, if need be, until he or she arrives. Or three, provide the selected songs without the lyrics. That's not, by the way, the end of the world. As it so happens one of Denver's best musicians—and best husbands—is playing the piano tonight. So. Those are my three. I'm open to others."

"I don't have any." Or did he? Pierce hadn't sung a note since the day Gabriel died. It would have been impossible to sing in the months that followed Gabriel's death, when Pierce's throat burned and his lungs were drowning. And in the ensuing years? Pierce had heard anew the songs of stone, of wood, of steel, of glass. He'd listened to those songs, and guided by that music, he'd created buildings that sang. But there'd been no music within him. No wish, no passion, to sing. Perhaps he couldn't even sing any longer. Regardless, Melissa's wedding was *not* the time to find out. "I am, however, quite comfortable excluding option two."

"I agree. So option one if possible? And otherwise three?"

"Sounds good. Although, Frances, isn't getting a singer at this late date on Valentine's night so unlikely that it's not even worth your time to try? Especially since we already have the best of the best at the baby grand?"

"Maybe. But I'm only planning to make one call, one try." Which she was making already, scanning her cell phone directory, finding the entry she wanted, pressing the command to dial. "I just have this feeling she might be avail—*hooray!* You're there. It's Frances, and have I got a gig for you, at your favorite of all places to sing, on the most romantic night of the year. . . . Yep. That's right. The Island. Tonight. The bride begins her march at eight, and she's really wedded, as it were, to beginning on time, so you'd need to start driving at, oh, right about *now*. It doesn't *matter* what you're wearing! You'll be in the alcove, completely out of sight. With Stephen, by the way, who'll cue you. So, yes? Can you? *Will* you? . . . Hello? Are you still there? . . . Yes? You will? *Wonderful.* You are a heroine of the first order. *Thank you, thank you, thank you.* What? Oh, 'Imagine Moonlight,' 'Dance with Me,' and 'One Heart.' Okay? *Great.* Drive carefully, please, but *start* driving—now."

Frances flipped her cell phone closed and smiled at Pierce. "We have option one."

"Terrific."

"As is she. In fact, Pierce Rourke, she—her voice—might just bring your days of eligible bachelorhood to a nuptial end. Simply having that voice at the ceremony, *blessing*

94

it . . . Stephen and I are actually considering renewing our vows."

"With Stephen as groom who'd accompany her?"

"No one. As Stephen won't tonight."

"She insists on singing a capella?"

"No. She doesn't *insist* on anything. But Stephen won't accompany her. He never does. As much as he loves playing, and as sensational as he is, when she sings he prefers to listen. You'll see, Pierce. Well, you'll *hear*."

*P*ierce did hear. How could he not? It was his gift to hear the music of the wind, the humming of flowers, the melodies of sky, of fire, of dawn, of sea.

On this Valentine's night, Liam Pierce Rourke heard the haunting carol of a human heart.

It touched him, pierced him, made him restless, more restless, and needy.

Needy.

Needing what?

To see her? Touch her? Make love to her? Or, an even greater intimacy, to *sing* with her?

Pierce wanted the seeing, the touching, the loving. Restlessly. And, astonishingly, he wanted the intimacy, the *involvement*, too.

With Anastasia.

Anastasia.

It was she who made him want, made him need, and who made him hear in the wedding singer's voice far more emotion, surely, than was truly there. It was *his* heart that was haunted. By Anastasia. The emotional carol he heard was his own.

Pierce had already decided when he'd call Anastasia, the hello again that would lead, he hoped, to more hello. On Monday, he'd decided. At school. He wouldn't shatter, even with gentleness, the courageous silence of her home.

And as for the wedding singer he could not see? The woman who gave song to the longings he felt?

Pierce would see her tonight. As the bride's grateful uncle, he'd thank her for her willingness to respond to Frances's last-minute plea, and for blessing his niece's marriage vows with a voice that was, by any measure, extraordinary.

Pierce's thank-you would happen soon. Melissa and Doug had just been pronounced husband and wife.

Usually, Val had explained, it was the newlyweds who led the recessional. The wedding party followed, then the parents and grandparents, then everyone else.

Melissa and Doug were departing from tradition. A decision made together, Val noted, as every decision about their wedding had been. If the groom didn't care about the details of celebrating his nuptial vows, what commitment would he have to the marriage itself?

The new couple would leave the chapel last. Like a host and hostess, they would watch their guests depart, beginning with the parents and grandparents they so dearly loved.

And here they came, those proud celebrants, happy basket cases all. Val's tears spilled, as did Thomas's, Lilah's, and Edward's, too. Douglas's side of the multigenerational parade of wedded bliss was comparably misty and smiling.

The bridesmaids and groomsmen followed, led by the beaming maid of honor. No tears glistened in Callie's eyes, just sun-bright joy. And, Pierce realized, an agenda: a silent yet eloquent message for him.

It was *so incredibly* nice of him—thank you so much, Uncle Pierce!—to have built this magical wedding place for Melissa. It was perfect, perfect, perfect!

The wedding guests flowed next, a leisurely drifting out of the chapel and toward the ballroom.

Pierce chose a different path, along a windowed hallway that linked foyer to alcove, and from which he could see that the wedding singer was already outside. It could only be her, clothed as she was in sweatshirt, tennis shoes, jeans.

A parka, unnecessary on this balmy night, was knotted at her waist. The parka would be unnecessary on any night, assuming she wore her hair as she did now, a luxuriant cape of moonlit gold.

She was leaving, forsaking the reception she would have been welcome to attend no matter her attire. Leaving *hurriedly*, despite the fact that Frances had enticed her to come to the Island with the reminder that this starlit moonscape was her favorite of all places to sing.

She seemed quite oblivious to this Venice in Denver, its shimmering glass, its sparkling fountains, its white-marble bridges, like gleaming pearl rainbows, arching over ponds of heated water and glittering ice.

She was hurrying, not marveling. Rushing. And now, as she crossed the final arch before veering toward the stairwell to the parking garage, she unknotted her parka, and slipped into its warmth.

She *didn't* veer toward the stairwell. Neither did she rush toward the forest where families of birds made their own homes that sang.

Instead, and as decisively as Pierce had separated from the flowing river of celebrants in search of her, she followed a path unfamiliar to most Island guests. Unfamiliar, unmarked, and illuminated only by starshine and moonglow.

The path was dark, despite the brilliance of the celestial lights, shadowed by the rows of teal green pine trees that had been planted by Pierce expressly to discourage visitors to this private place.

His private place.

She wasn't discouraged. She had purpose. Destination.

The pine-fragrant path ended at the lake, and the lightless cottage nearby. Lightless, as always. And lonely, empty, locked.

But the lake was aglow, glistening, champagne ice sprinkled with silver stars. And beyond that shining mirror of frozen water? There lay, on the opposite shore, a gently sloping field of snow, a welcoming meadow, the only one, in the wreath of cliffs that encircled the lake.

The snowfield on this sparkling night was the silken gown of a heavenly bride, and the crystal mountains, in starlit blue, glowed like proud parents in the velvet sky.

The lake was, Pierce knew, quite frozen. The recent

balminess had melted only the glistening surface of its thick frosting of ice.

The determined wedding singer seemed to know, too, the frosting was solid. Or perhaps she simply had no fear.

She walked fifteen feet onto the shining mirror, then twenty, thirty, forty. At which point she stopped decisively, her destination finally reached.

She had come, apparently, to view the snowfield from precisely there, that spot of ice. She was marveling now at the view—as, Pierce realized, he was marveling at her.

And was she listening, as he was? Did she hear, this gifted songstress, the music of mountains and moonglow? Of snow and stars?

She was definitely listening, Pierce decided.

He imagined a smile. And hoped for a song.

But she was silent.

And fragile, he thought. Lonely.

And so very alone.

He stepped from snow-rock shore onto glistening ice. Slippery lake. He was far less surefooted, he discovered, than was she.

His journey was surprisingly silent, a hushed glide from the fading scent of pines to the fragrance of violets. *Violets*. And to a luxuriant mane that was sable, not gold. It had merely captured moonbeams, embracing and treasuring their golden light.

Violets. Sable. The haunting carol of a human heart. His own. And hers?

"Anastasia."

She didn't startle. Nor did she turn.

"Liam," she whispered to the tableau of snow and stars she had come to see. "I mean *Pierce*."

She'd learned a little about him, apparently. The wrong things. The architect—and man—named Pierce who was uncompromising in his commitment to quality in his designs, and comparably uncompromising in his commitment to remaining uncommitted, uninvolved, in the quality physical relationships he enjoyed.

That was Pierce Rourke. But . . .

"I'm Liam, Anastasia." *Liam for you. With you.* "Anastasia?"

She turned to the gentleness. Him.

"Are you okay?" he asked.

"I'm *fine*." She swiped at her watery eyes. "It's just that this place . . ."

"Makes you cry."

"In a good way. It's so beautiful. It's my dream, Liam." *Mine too.* "Your dream?"

"My lovely dream déjà vu. *This* place. Right here. And exactly *like* this, when, in my dream, I'm here at night."

"And when your dreams bring you here during the day?"

"Oh, it's a busy place then, buzzing with life, with laughter, with the sounds of skaters and their skates."

"Good sounds?"

"To me, yes. Happy and gay. And the only clue that the skaters are here. I never see them at all."

"Do you skate?"

"In my dream only. And only at night." She smiled. "I'm quite the skater then, a ballerina on ice beneath the stars,

100

spinning, twirling, reaching for the moon." Her smile vanished. "How's that for madness?"

"It sounds like gladness, Anastasia. Not madness."

"Gladness," she echoed, and shivered.

"Are you cold?"

"No." It had been a tremble of warmth. A quiver of safeness, of gladness, *of madness.* "I got here in time."

"Meaning?"

"This spot is an antidote to the coldness." *The only antidote, Liam Rourke. Until you. And not nearly as potent, Liam Rourke, as you.*

"You expect to get cold when you sing?"

"Yes. Always. And I usually get the headaches, too."

"But still you sing."

"I *have* to sing."

The Passion of Miss Finch.

"Your singing is . . ."

"Your Island is . . ."

The impending praises of their separate passions came as one, a flawless duet.

He smiled. And she smiled. And as one, and in perfect harmony, they whispered, "Thanks."

"We could walk across the lake," Pierce said.

"You mean now?"

"That's what I meant. But it could be another time. Anytime." *All the time.* "We could try it with skates if you like."

Pierce saw the wishing yes.

And the wistful no.

"I wonder what happens to a dream when you get too close."

"Maybe," Pierce murmured, "it gets even better."

They glided closer, then, to a different dream. He began the journey, touching her so gently, but she was gliding with him, she was the joyful ballerina after all, the intrepid skater who danced and twirled.

Her cheeks warmed to his touch, and her eyes glowed yes with wanting, yes with wishing, yes with wonder, and her lips opened to his, welcoming, wanting, wishing. Yes. Yes.

Then no.

No.

"I can't do this. It's madness, Liam."

"It's gladness, Anastasia."

"No. *No.*"

"Talk to me. Please."

"I *am* going mad."

"Then so am I. If this is madness, Anastasia, I'll gladly go with you."

"No, Liam. You don't understand. I *will* go mad. It will happen to me as it has happened to women in my family for generations. *All* women in my family. Always. And young. In their early thirties. With death, the lucky ones, by the time they're thirty-five."

"That's not going to happen to you." His eyes were fierce and tender, ice and fire, dark and sure.

He wasn't going to *let* it happen to her, his glittering gaze asserted. End of worry. And beginning again of the dream.

For a glorious moment the lost princess was lost in that promise, persuaded by it. He could, after all, vanquish her most pounding headache, melt her most frigid cold. Why not alter her destiny, too?

He wanted to. She saw how much. And that he would if he could. But even this green-eyed magician, with his fearsome power, his tender will, could not make disappear this inevitable fate.

"It is going to happen to me, Liam. It *will*. And soon. I'm already thirty-one. The dementia will come first, the consequence of an Alzheimer's-like deterioration, then when the damage is advanced, the insanity will begin."

"There must be something."

"No," Anastasia whispered to the most potent of all somethings. *Even you can't prevent it, Liam. Even you.*

Pierce heard her no, and saw it in the wistful shadows of her bright blue eyes. Wistful, yet decisive. Accepting and calm. "How long have you known?"

"Since I was fifteen. The same year," she elaborated softly, "I discovered I could sing. I've always believed the two were linked, that singing was something I would have in exchange for what I would not. Could not."

Like wishes, Pierce thought. Like dreams. Anastasia might be accepting of such a fate. Resigned to it. He was not. "You've been followed by neurologists for the past sixteen years?"

"Yes. Closely."

"And they've done all the genetic tests?"

"There aren't any genetic tests to do. Not yet. There *is* a genetic marker, some heritable time bomb in our familial DNA. The chromosomal mapping just hasn't been done. Which is true of a number of similar familial dementia syndromes. There's really very little need, in my instance, to devote much time to a search for the marker. The family history is persuasive."

"I'm not persuaded."

Oh, but you must be. "Boston's leading neurologists are, as is Denver's best."

"This is why you felt you should be evaluated by Thomas. Even more than because of the drugs."

"Yes. Although I was concerned about both. I'd never worked with children and wanted to be very certain the girls would be safe with me. They would be, I reasoned, if Hazel Traphagen's faculty and parents were informed, aware, on guard."

"On guard, Anastasia? Against you?"

"Against my madness. In the event it came on acutely, as my mother's supposedly did."

"Supposedly."

"I was eight when she died. My memories are of loss, not of madness. I was told her psychosis came on suddenly, virtually overnight. But every specialist I've seen, your brother-in-law included, doubts that's true. It may have *seemed* that way. But the signs of dementia had undoubtedly been present for months, maybe years. She might have detected the signs herself, as Alzheimer's patients often can, had she known or been willing to look."

"You've looked, been looking, since you were fifteen."

"Yes. And until that glass of lemonade I believed I was all right. Doing just fine. Which I *was.* The same me I'd known all my life. I was in touch with the world, its noises and its news, and what headaches I had made sense, and unless I'd underestimated the layers needed for a winter day in Boston, I was never cold. But since July . . ."

"You said the dementia precedes the madness."

"It does. And there's a consensus among the neurologists I've seen that even if LSD had been sprinkled in the lemonade, it wouldn't have accelerated my underlying disease. Our familial decay is genetically predetermined and unaffected by drugs. LSD can, of course, precipitate fullblown psychosis in patients with other mental illnesses, so if I happen to have one of those latent psychoses, too . . ."

"You don't."

"Don't I? What if not madness would compel me to create a world of silence, and then listen in the crazy belief there's something I'm supposed to hear?"

"Gladness might do it."

"Gladness?"

"Do you hear music in the silence?"

"Yes," she whispered. "Sometimes. Here, Liam. I hear music *here*. Do you?"

"Yes."

"Do you sing?"

"Not for years. Decades. But I want to sing, Anastasia. Here. With you."

Say yes, Anastasia. Say yes to that intimacy.

"I can't. *I can't.* It isn't . . ."

"Possible? Sure it is. Admittedly, my voice was never what yours is, never so extraordinary, and what's left is very likely rusted with disuse. Or did you mean, Anastasia, that it isn't right—fair? wise?—for us to get involved? If so, it's too late. I am involved. And, I think, you are, too."

"You weren't *listening.*"

"You know I was listening. You know, *you know,* I heard every word." Every word. Each one a plunging knife of ice. No wonder she shivered. No wonder she froze. "I am involved, Anastasia. I want to be."

"But it's not what *I* want!"

"Then so be it, if you can tell me you'd feel the same way if the situation were reversed." *If you, lovely songstress, had inherited all gifts for music, and it was a bomb in my DNA that relentlessly ticked its fatal dirge.*

Anastasia couldn't tell him that. Could not.

But the situation wasn't reversed, and the lovely dream déjà vu, the one good consequence of her poisoned lemonade, now seemed its worst. For here, on this island of her dreams, was a more magnificent dream, the most magnificent one. Him. Liam. This man who wanted her.

If this is madness, he'd said, I'll gladly go with you.

He was saying it still.

"I have to go, Liam. Let me go."

He wasn't holding her. Not physically. And she escaped, his wistful, willful princess, the invisible bonds of his wishes. Of his love.

She glided, like the skater she was in her dream. Glided. Glided.

Away.

EIGHT

*G*iselle Trouveau's Carmel Valley studio was a meadow's walk from her Carmel Valley home. The studio was the larger of the two structures. Much larger. And not merely because the artist needed space in which to gather molten glass from flaming fire and twirl it, spin it, gentle it into shape.

Giselle's studio was where she spent most of her life. Chose to. Wanted to.

Loved to.

Giselle's melting furnace could have come from Murano, where glass had been crafted for a thousand years. So too from the Venetian isle her blowpipes, her mavers, her recipes for colors pure and true. And, as Italian glassmakers had done for centuries, Giselle kept a pan of pasta water simmering on the stove.

There were no windows in Giselle's studio, or clocks, or computers, or phones, or fax—no way to discern dawn from dusk, night from day, winter from spring.

Giselle slept in her studio when she worked, and soaked her weary muscles in its bath. And when an inner chime inevitably sounded? A signal that it was time to emerge from her volcanic cocoon?

With a sense of interest, she would. Interest. But not urgency. Not on a personal level at least. Giselle was ever mindful of the tragedies that befell strangers. Mourned for them.

But no private crises would be awaiting her. She had no family. No lovers. No tight-knit circle of friends. No circle at all.

There would be no professional crises, either. There didn't exist, in her view, authentic emergencies when it came to selling art.

Whenever she had pieces to sell, Giselle simply made a local call, to the Ocean Crest Gallery, where, from the first, her creations had been welcomed as if she were an established sculptress not an utter unknown.

Giselle sold exclusively with Ocean Crest still. Exclusively, and around the world. And as for the commissioned pieces she was asked to do? The architectural installations for homes, opera houses, palaces, hotels? She created such installations for Pierce Rourke only.

Pierce. Who'd left a phone message, she discovered when she emerged from her studio on this February day. She'd been working for a week. It was noon, FOX News informed her. Thursday. The nineteenth.

The nineteenth. The day, the date, of such memories for her. Of destiny. Of love.

Pierce's message, her only one, had been left on Saturday night, Valentine's night, at 12:22 A.M.

At 1:22 A.M. his time.

She'd told him years ago that he could call her anytime. She silenced her home phone whenever she was there and sleeping. If she wasn't home, she advised him without apology, it might be days before she checked her messages and returned his call.

There'd been many such times. A days-old, week-old message from Pierce. But never, she thought, one that had actually been left in the middle of the night.

The Carillon Square and Commons project was in its final stages, this message revealed. The Commons would be a lake, Pierce said, not a park after all.

It would be frozen, the Carillon lake, for ice-skating, that gliding gaiety, year-round. There'd be a lake within the lake, an island of water at its westernmost tip. It was there, in the watery island within the sea of ice, that Pierce would place the glass fountain she would make.

He wanted violets, like the ones that bloomed on her chandelier gift to the school. And rising from the center of the bouquet, he wanted a skater. She would spin, Pierce said, and dance and twirl as she reached for the moon.

Fountain and skater both would twirl, he added. Separately and together.

Giselle listened to Pierce's message twice, confirming on

the second pass her surprising impression from the first. Not only had Pierce been precise about what he wanted, but he'd sounded unyielding as well.

It wasn't that Pierce never voiced opinions about the glass installations she might make to complement his designs. Of course he did. Often. Just as without the slightest hesitation, and within moments of seeing it, she'd said of his Island, *Venice*.

But from the beginning of their collaboration, the architectural art had been his and the glass art had been hers.

True, the collaboration existed only because of Pierce. The celebrated architect had called her out of the blue. His first Wind Chimes, the Denver one, was nearing completion, and he needed a chime for its lobby.

He hadn't even been thinking glass. But when his Alta Vista search for "wind+chime" found a chime of cherry blossoms on the Ocean Crest Gallery web page . . .

He would install two Giselle Trouveau wind chimes, he decided when he saw the photograph. A forty-foot fall of petals for the hotel, a twenty-foot one for the Towers. The individual blossoms would need to be commensurately enlarged, of course. Massive. Heavy. Huge.

No, Giselle had told him. Without telling him why. She worked alone. Had to. In her private world of glass and flames.

She'd make life-size cherry blossoms for him only. Yes, thousands upon thousands, fluttering, chiming, in every shade of pink, of rose, of orchid, of pearl.

She'd been unyielding, she'd had no choice, and the famously uncompromising architect had quite amiably acquiesced.

Over the years Pierce had pushed her to create pieces she'd never believed she could. He needed a fountain, he'd tell her, or a statue, a mural, a floor-to-ceiling sconce.

Giselle had created those sculptures—massive, heavy, huge—as if crafting an immense jigsaw puzzle, piece by tiny glassy piece, sealed as seamlessly by fire as if she'd had the help, as many glass artists did, of a strong and many-handed team.

Pierce would usually specify the category of installation he'd like her to do. Chandelier, fountain, statue, vase. But sometimes, when the project was architecturally the way he wanted it to be, he'd simply say, "Your turn, Giselle."

The Carillon project was, apparently, the way Pierce wanted it—would be, once the lake was made. And Pierce's vision of *her* finishing touch for *his* lake of ice was magnificent.

But still . . .

Pierce answered her call on the sixth ring. Giselle had decided, as the rings went unanswered, that there was significant background noise in Denver, with Pierce, on this Thursday afternoon. The sound of creating from scratch a brand-new lake.

But when he answered, she heard only silence. The sound, knowing Pierce, of water in his already carved lake turning to ice.

"The skater's a she?" Giselle greeted. And hearing more silence, "Pierce? It's Giselle."

"I know. Sorry. I guess I'm a little distracted. The answer is yes. The skater's a she."

"And she's skating alone?"

So alone, Pierce thought. As she was. His lovely skater. Twirling with grace in her private dream, with courage in her private hell, and reaching for the moon for as long as she could. "Yes. Alone."

Pierce was not, Giselle realized, going to insert even an "I was thinking" into his vision, *his mandate*, of what he wanted from her. Much less an "assuming you agree." And there wasn't the slightest chance of hearing "It's entirely your call."

It wasn't her call. Not entirely. *Not at all.*

"Pierce?"

"Yes?"

"What's wrong?"

"Wrong?"

"You sound . . ." *lost. Sad.* Lost? Sad? *Pierce?* "Something."

"I am, Giselle." The quiet confession came with a sigh. "Something."

Something personal, she realized. Private. Which, despite the artistic closeness they shared, their relationship was not. Had never been.

But this was February 19, the anniversary for her of love.

And gratitude.

"Here's *something*," she said softly. "Thank you, Pierce Rourke. I've never really said that before."

"Giselle? You've said it at least a million times, all un-necessary, and that was just in the first year."

"And you've said it, too—incredibly, unnecessarily, at least a million times."

"And didn't we agree years ago to impose a permanent moratorium on such exchanges?"

"We did. Yes. But this is a personal thank-you, Pierce. And it's long overdue. So thank you, belatedly, for putting up with me. It can't have been easy. I know. I lived with it. *Me.* I know very well how difficult I was. Brittle. Hostile. Wary. Tense."

"Unhappy," he said quietly.

"That's a gracious way of putting it."

"That's all I ever thought, Giselle. That you were un-happy. Were. Past tense, as of your return-to-Venice trip. True?"

"True. My newfound happiness must have been a relief for you."

"For you."

"Yes. Definitely. Pierce? Is there anything I can do? For the 'something,' whatever it is?"

"Make me a skater, Giselle. Make her dance with joy."

$\mathcal{G}$iselle promised as their conversation ended that she would do just that.

And, Pierce vowed as he returned to silence, I will make a home for Anastasia.

He was in that home, the cottage on the Island with

113

the view of her dream. She could live here as long as she liked.

Live here. Sing here.

Go insane here.

Die here.

She could be alone. Here. As she wanted to be. Until, that is, she needed him. She wouldn't know he was with her then. But he would be.

And maybe they would sing.

He would protect her. Care for her. Make certain she was warm, fed, unfrightened, without pain. And he wouldn't let her fall, his solitary skater, wouldn't let her drown when springshine thinned to gossamer delicacy the lake's wintertime ice.

Anastasia lived already in a home designed by Pierce. A condo at the Canterbury a mile from the school. He'd had no trouble finding her home address. Her home phone.

She was listed. In the event, he imagined, some little girl wanted to talk.

Anastasia Finch was not in hiding. Not from the girls.

And from him? No. She trusted him to leave unshattered the silence of her Canterbury home.

Pierce called her at school and reached Mrs. Holt, to whom the librarian's phone had been forwarded.

"I'm afraid she's not here," Mrs. Holt said following the usual politenesses.

"But will be returning soon?"

"No. At least she'd *better* not be! We've sent her home for the day. What's left of it. She has that terrible cold that's going around. Everyone has it. Except me—I'm either immune or a carrier!—and of course Callie, who simply can't be bothered, it seems, ever to be ill. But our dear librarian *is* ill. And because of this Grace thing she needs to rest. To *recover*."

"This Grace thing? You mean the article for book club?"

"See! You've heard about it, too. Well, but you *would* have, wouldn't you, because of Callie?"

Pierce didn't answer her question. He merely issued a command. "No one's blaming Anastasia that the article was selected."

"Anastasia," Mrs. Holt echoed. "No. They're not. At least not anymore. That brouhaha lasted only until Monday afternoon. By then the entire school knew anyway. Erin has sisters, you see, in grades two and five."

"So the Grace thing is?"

"Where to go from here. There will be an all-school book club. That's a given. Scheduled, at the moment, for a week from tomorrow. And, at the moment, Miss . . . Ana will be moderating it. Which means that despite her terrible cold, and all the extraneous wear and tear, she's been spending her every after-school hour surfing the web, or Net, or whatever it is one surfs. She *has* to because that's what the girls are all doing, visiting the Finding Grace web site, reading the original newspaper accounts, studying the gallery of photos of Loganville, et cetera, et cetera. That's more than enough for her to do in her spare time. *Fatiguing* enough. But add to that the numerous administrative meetings she's felt obliged to attend."

"Meetings because of Grace?"

"Yes. During the course of the week—goodness, is it

still only Thursday?—there've been proposals ranging from a field trip to Loganville, with book club to be held at the library there, to inviting some of the key folks there to come here for something like a nationally televised show-and-tell."

"A what?"

"I know. It's sort of beyond inappropriate, isn't it? But there's the Aunt Dinah *hook*, you see, and the fact that Dinah's sister—Erin, Lisa, and Jenna's mother—has that local talk show herself. Which doesn't mean she's opposed to *co*hostessing with Oprah. When last I checked, though, *your* sister had put a fairly definitive kibosh on any misguided plans to broadcast the worried faces of our lovely little girls. But you can see the kind of week it's been for Ana. I've told her to turn off her phone, we'll come get her if we need her, and sleep until morning."

"Do you expect her in then?"

"Expect, yes. Want, no. Which I told her, as did Mrs. Fairchild. We'd like her to take a long weekend. She's agreed to call before coming in. May I give her a message when she does?"

"Please." *Tell her I hope she was able to sleep, to dream, and that her terrible cold doesn't mean she's terribly cold, and . . .* "If you would tell her that I called? And have her call me at her convenience? It's not urgent, tell her. And it's about the Island, not Grace."

NINE

*G*iselle spent until evening envisioning the glass sculpture she'd promised to make for Pierce.

Trying to envision it.

She kept seeing two skaters, not one. Yes, Pierce's *she* was there. His joyful skater reaching for the moon. But she wasn't alone. True, Giselle's *he* wasn't touching her. Indeed he was far away, at the other tip of the icy lake, watching her, loving her, so proud of her.

As he'd promised he would always be. Giselle's *he*.

So how to keep her promise to Pierce? To reconcile their conflicting visions? By making him, the second skater, invisible . . . as *he* was. Giselle would know he was there, and her ballerina on ice, her twirling dancer atop violets,

117

would know it, too—and she'd be warmed by it, filled by it, blessed by it. Too.

Night had fallen by the time Giselle glanced through her seven days of accumulated mail. The light bill, due ten days hence, was her most personal communiqué. She'd pay it before returning to flames—and love and ice—in the event she remained in her studio in excess of ten days.

She'd received a number of catalogues, a coupon mailer from a consortium of local merchants, and two magazines to which she subscribed.

Architectural Digest and *People*.

Giselle didn't recognize the girl on the cover of *People*. But she smiled, without realizing she was smiling, at the lovely face.

And Giselle frowned, knowing she was frowning, as she read the horror that had befallen such innocence.

And when she came to the photo-booth snapshots from which the cover photo had been taken? The two frames of the original four that Grace's best friend Dinah had kept all these years?

Giselle, too, had a two-frame photo strip in her possession. One she'd kept all these years. Since that January in New Orleans.

That January, a calendar of which appeared at the top of the following page. The missing week was framed in a Valentine pink, and the caption below queried *People* readers everywhere, Where were *you* during these seven days? Where were *they*?

They. Troy and Grace. Monster and victim. Man and girl.

The girl Giselle had known, cared for. Cared about. As she cared about her still.

Giselle's hands, so confident in their creations of glass, trembled as she fanned the pages to the article's final paragraph where, it had been promised, details for sharing information would be.

Giselle had information to share, and she would share it with . . .

Garek McIntyre. Her invisible skater. The man whose dark blue eyes watched her still. Proudly, lovingly. Watched, but did not wait. Her skater had his own life to live.

Her skater. Her Garek.

He had been hers once, for those enchanted hours on this date, *this* date, three years ago in Venice . . .

*I*t was Carnivale in Venice.

Carnivale. "Farewell to flesh." The feasting before the fasting that was Lent.

According to historians, the first Venetian Carnivale had been celebrated in 1094. During that initial gala fortnight, and for the seven ensuing centuries until Napoléon, masked Venetian noblewomen had found love with lowly gondoliers, and costumed peasant girls had bewitched and bedded lofty doges, and courtesans, being courtesans, had enjoyed passion and pretense with whomever they pleased.

Carnivale glittered in Venice still. Again. After almost two hundred years of slumber imposed by the French conqueror who'd forbidden his new subjects from wearing disguises of any kind. Ever.

Disguise flourished again in the City of Canals. Masks and costumes. Mystery and charade. Secrecy and seduction.

And celebration above all.

Giselle planned a private celebration, the end of all charade, and a new beginning, she promised herself, *the* new beginning at last.

She'd believed she'd begun when she left Venice nine years earlier. Left *him*. Armande. And in many ways she had begun then. She'd found—no, she'd achieved—success and solitude. Precious treasures both.

Success and solitude. But not serenity. Not yet.

Serenity wasn't going to find her, she realized. She'd have to search for it, work for it, achieve it, too.

She journeyed within, examining with unwavering determination every parcel of emotional baggage she'd carried with her from Venice when she'd left. It was an amazing cargo, she discovered. Massive and weighty. Enough to sink the most seaworthy vessel in the Venetian Lagoon.

And when Giselle peered into the suitcases, satchels, duffel bags, and trunks? She saw anger, loathing, disgust. For him *and for her.* No wonder, despite her relief at getting away from him, she had yet to feel truly calm, truly free.

She felt quite the opposite, in fact: brittle, wary, hostile, tense.

She needed to lug the entire pallet of impedimenta back to Venice, where it had been so meticulously packed, and toss it piece by weighty piece into the deep blue sea.

Giselle was an invited guest at this year's Carnivale. She'd wanted to be invited, had orchestrated it. True, the initial invitation had been an unprompted surprise. An unexpected honor. A request to attend the international art exhibition in the Giardini di Castello.

The world-renowned spectacular would be held in summer. As always. All expenses would be assumed by the Biennale, as would all costs and every care in returning both Giselle and her glassy wonders safely home.

The exhibition organizers knew that Giselle Trouveau never appeared with her art. Appeared at all, even in photographs. But as the reclusive sculptress surely knew, it was tradition in summer in the Castello Gardens for every participant artist to be on display as well, just an hour or two a day, for smiling exchanges with patrons who flocked to the exhibition from around the world.

Giselle had declined to attend the summertime extravaganza with regret, citing conflicts. She could come in February, though. During Carnivale. It was during Carnivale, Giselle knew, that she and her baggage needed to return.

She'd *love* to come during Carnivale, in fact. And, she said, she'd be delighted to craft a special collection of masks for the occasion.

She'd need only a place to display her Masquerade Collection, nothing grand, and a little publicity, too? And she'd be happy to be available to the public on whatever schedule her Venetian hosts might choose.

And so it was, and far beyond her wildest imaginings, that the Festival of Masks was born. For her. For her art. And because she certainly did *not* object, other mask artists, although none in glass, would be invited to display their creations, too—their Carnivale extravagances of feathers and beads, sequins and silk, decoupage and papier-mâché.

A temporary pavilion would be constructed in Piazza San Marco. Yes, *there*. And as for the little bit of publicity she'd hoped for? Invitations would be mailed to every art patron that mattered. The Biennale had such an august list. And Ocean Crest Gallery had relevant names as well, of collectors and would-be collectors of Giselle's work.

So here she was on this final day of the Festival of Masks, this Shrove Tuesday, this Mardi Gras, this February 19 in Venice—La Serenissima—the most serene.

She would be most serene, she'd promised herself, once she'd seen Armande.

Bonjour, Armande. *Adieu,* Armande.

Hello. Good-bye. With carefully chosen words in between. Giselle had chosen those words and rehearsed them to perfection. Contemptuous words calmly spoken, their message of disdain crystal-clear.

But the words she was planning were imploring as well. *Imploring.* She wanted Armande to understand what he'd done to her, to acknowledge his role as she acknowledged hers. And to apologize? Yes. And more: to ask forgiveness, beg forgiveness, of her.

Giselle discovered on her return to La Serenissima that Armande was quite superfluous.

Serenity was already here, just waiting for her to claim it, completely within her control.

She was perfectly capable of tossing the unwanted baggage into the Lagoon, wasn't she? All by herself?

Yes. It was her baggage after all. And she was so capable. So strong. And what had seemed impossibly heavy, trunks so laden that she and Armande would have to strain together to shove them to water's edge, were feathery light.

As was she. Light. Floating. Unweighted in this city she once had loved, this enchantment of watery streets and gardens of walls.

Giselle loved Venice. Again. Before even seeing Armande. She didn't need to see him. Ever. She needed nothing from him. No apologies, no heavy lifting, nothing.

And as for the forgiveness to be implored? Giselle forgave herself. Venice forgave her. The canals, the wisteria, the clear winter light.

But she *would* see Armande. The Parisian entrepreneur, and patron of the arts, would have received the engraved invitation that she'd wanted, planned, for him to receive.

Armande would be appearing any moment now. The pavilion doors would be closing in fifteen minutes. At three. He'd drop by as if an afterthought, as if, during that quarter hour, he really had nothing better to do.

And here he was, right on cue. Giselle felt so calm when she saw him. She knew him so well. Who he was. What he was. All that he was.

She'd even known the words he would speak, and that he'd do so in his excellent English, not his native French.

They'd spoken French during their eleven years together. Armande had deigned to share his beautiful language with her, a gift from him to her, a condescending intimacy—no matter that her French was as flawless as his.

But it was English for her now, this woman, this *American* who'd dared to leave him.

"You've done well, Gigi. Quite a little talent. How fortunate I brought you to Venice."

She'd expected him to take credit for her success, and waited in serene silence for his next perfectly forecast taunt.

"Did you bed them, pet?"

"Who, Armande?" Giselle countered with exquisite calm in flawless French. "The glass masters of Murano? Of course I did. How else, but with seduction, could I learn their secrets?"

How else? Precisely as she had learned. By watching, as tourists were encouraged to do; observing the master gaffers and their apprentice sons at furnace face in the glass factories of Murano.

The maestros and their sons. Murano and glass were for men. Only. And for the mothers and daughters of the Venetian Lagoon? Lace.

"You're lying," Armande accused in response to her assertion that she'd learned in bed the secrets of making glass . . . a skill once so protected that to reveal its mysteries was to risk certain death.

A feathery lightness lifted her shoulders in a delicate shrug. "Believe what you wish, Armande."

Armande wished to believe something else.

"Look at you," he scoffed. "Your clothes. Your hair. You've become a *man*, Giselle."

Armande's disdainful gaze raked from her short coppery locks—stylish, functional, *her*—to the ebony flow of tunic and trousers, belted in moonlight, to her winter coat, long and charcoal, nearby.

Except for this gala time in Venice, when costumes were de rigueur, Giselle's look was distinctly Venetian: sophisticated elegance in gondola black, the bewitching hue and promise of midnight.

The new Giselle, the one who belonged to herself not to Armande, wore only clothes she loved. And although she needed no embellishments beyond her copper hair, her whiskey eyes, her gardenia skin, the artist accented her night-sky ensembles with imaginative splashes of gold or silver, of amethyst or ruby, of coral *and* pearl.

"What a waste," Armande informed the woman, so far from a man, who'd met even this insult with infuriating calm. "I'd planned to invite you to the palazzo tonight. My gala will be, as it always is, the city's most lavish. It might have been a profitable night for you. More in a few hours than these glass trinkets could bring in many years."

"Don't bother to invite me, Armande. I wouldn't come."

"But maybe you should. Maybe it's not too late. I hadn't envisioned *us* together, not after the way you left me. But I could remind you what it is to be a woman. I could teach you again. I would do that for you."

Armande curled a possessive finger in her coppery hair, then traced a path from temple to cheek to mouth. Giselle didn't flinch, didn't move.

"Come with me to the palazzo, Gigi. Come *now.*"

This was the place in the angry words she'd rehearsed where she would have told him how loathsome he was, and would have implored him to acknowledge such truth.

125

But now . . .

"*Adieu*, Armande."

His smile was tight, mean. "*Adieu*, Gigi?"

"*Oui.*"

Armande's other fingers joined the one that had been resting on her mouth, reinforcements that claimed her entire jaw as tightly, as meanly, as his smile.

Giselle neither moved nor flinched. Still.

Finally, with a punishing twist, his imprisoning grasp fell away.

Farewell to flesh.

"Giselle." The new voice was quiet, commanding, intimate, male. And his eyes, so blue, gazed at her as if Armande didn't exist, never had. "I've been waiting, my love. So patiently. Your many admirers never want to let you go. Who can blame them? But it's my time now. *Our* time. Isn't it?"

"Yes," she whispered to the intimate stranger. "It is your time. Our time. Armande? *Adieu. Vraiment. Adieu.*"

Giselle didn't look at Armande as she bade him good-bye. *Truly.* Good-bye. But she heard his footfalls as he strode away.

"Thank you," she said as footfalls—and Armande— faded. "Thank you for rescuing me."

"You rescued yourself. Didn't you? Hadn't you already?"

"Yes. I did. I had. You heard what we were saying?"

"No. I just saw it. He wants you."

"Yes."

"And you want, very much, for him to stay away. Is that possible? Will he?"

"Stay away? Certainly. In the nine years since we parted, he's made no attempt to contact me. But Armande is very big on winning. Seeing me today reminded him that he doesn't always get to."

"You wanted to remind him."

The blue eyes saw so much.

"Who *are* you?"

"Garek McIntyre. One of those many admirers I mentioned. I promised myself I wasn't going to leave Venice without meeting you."

"Leave Venice?"

"My flight to Geneva departs from Marco Polo at ten tonight. If you're in the mood, we could walk for a while."

TEN

*T*hey walked for hours in the moody city of romance. Talked for hours. But Giselle and Garek did not touch. Never touched. Not with hands, not with lips, not with mouths.

Early in their wanderings, Garek told her how old he was, forty to her thirty-seven, and what he was: an attorney who practiced contract law in Chicago, and a husband.

Giselle learned, as they walked, as they talked, as they touched without touching, *who* he was.

Their journey began in Piazza San Marco, where she was, where her masks were, where the crowds were. The famous square, the renowned drawing room of Europe, was the site on this winter afternoon of the world's most grand masquerade ball.

All the traditional Carnivale celebrants had come to the piazza. La Buatta, the domino, roamed the festive square, his cape black, his three-cornered hat jaunty, his mask a ghostly white. Harlequins roamed, cavorted, too, as did Il Dottore, the doctor, and Punchinello, the hunchback, and Pierrot, the clown.

Then there were the modern-day revelers, dressed from brocade to chiffon, from Renaissance to New Age, from warmth against the winter chill to near nudity—save for their elaborate masks, the essence of Carnivale, the lavish guises that enabled one to see *everything* without ever truly *being* seen.

Garek and Giselle walked through Piazza San Marco and far away, to places in the labyrinth of canals and bridges that were quiet on this festive night. And undisguised, as they were. Unmasked. Unveiled.

Seeing . . . and being seen.

A pearl moon cast its lustrous glow as Giselle told Garek about Armande.

"I was his mistress."

"You fell in love with a married man. It happens."

"Yes. It does. But our liaison had nothing to do with love. It was arranged."

"Arranged?"

"And very French. Very Parisian. Very Gigi."

*   *   *

*I*t was Monique Jabot who named the newborn Giselle, and Monique who within days of the baby girl's birth bestowed the nickname Gigi. The endearment had special meaning for Monique, a symbol of her own affection for the fictional Parisian girl who'd found love while in training to become a mistress.

Monique had also named, *re*named, Gigi's mother, bayou-born Amy Louise Trent. She'd become, just months before her daughter's birth, Aimee Trouveau.

Monique was French. Parisian. By age forty-two, when Giselle was born, Monique had already enjoyed—until his death—twenty-five years as the pampered consort of one of France's wealthiest men.

Her lover's wife had known of Monique. *Naturellement.* She'd known Monique herself. And she'd approved of her husband's mistress, as had his sons, his daughters, his elite circle of powerful friends.

This was the way civilizations thrived. Bloodlines were protected, pedigrees preserved, and wealth was neither tainted nor scattered by the unsavory venom of divorce.

The wives were happy. They had lovers, too. And the husbands were willing fathers, good fathers, and families remained intact.

Monique's lover lavished her with gifts throughout their union, and at his death with a bequest that, as substantial as it was, placed in no peril the inheritance left to his children and wife.

Monique received a small fortune in cash and a mansion in New Orleans. They'd seen the French Quarter dwelling together during a business trip to the States. To her surprise, Frenchwoman that she was, Monique had been enamored not only of the mansion but of the Big Easy itself.

Still, Monique Jabot couldn't imagine living in America. Until her lover died. Paris wasn't the same without him. *Europe* wasn't the same.

Monique was willing to share with the young women of her new country her secrets of happiness, the way to live a truly delicious life.

Her New Orleans mansion would become a school, *une académie*, for mistresses.

The enlightenment of American women—and of American men—was a challenge. Divorce was so easy, as was sex, and given that everything in America was so new, two centuries young at most, there weren't even the sacred bloodlines to protect.

But Monique was a true believer. An impassioned one. She lectured her handpicked sorority of mistresses-to-be on all manner of things. Manners included. And elegance, culture, class, style.

And sex? Never. Her pupils were chosen for their sensual beauty. Their exquisite femininity. No instruction need be given such women. They knew the weapons in their arsenals. Besides, such explicit discussions were gauche, vulgar, crude.

Her elegantly appointed mansion was *not* a brothel, Monique explained with exasperated patience to her trainees, her clients, and the metropolitan police. The only intimate relations permitted in her home would be with men *she* might choose to entertain.

Yes. Money changed hands, though never between Monique and her lovers. But for quality time with her quality girls? Absolutely. A great deal of money. Wasn't such entrepreneurship the American way?

There was no payment, however, for sex. No *charge* for same. And correct her if she was wrong, *s'il vous plaît*, but wasn't sex between consenting adults permissible in the New World?

Monique's "escort" service, so called because it was a term American men understood, was wildly profitable. But save for its revenues, it wasn't even close to what she'd hoped.

Her vision of introducing American culture to a system of revered mistresses and flourishing families hadn't worked. No long-term relationships had evolved. Not one in eighteen years. True, there'd been marriages. Several. But since severed families floundered in the matrimonial wakes, Monique regarded those unions as failures.

Monique was in search of a disciple still, an ideal *and idolized* mistress who would validate Monique's life by imitating it precisely.

Monique pinned her hopes, still, on one of her first recruits. Aimee Trouveau. Née Amy Louise Trent.

Monique had spotted the runaway teen during Mardi Gras. Amy had been stoned at the time and prostituting herself, absently nodding yes to whatever was being offered—money or drugs—as her bedazzled gaze remained fixed on the costumed gaiety of Bourbon Street.

Stoned, prostituting herself, and four months pregnant.

Monique took Amy to her mansion, gave her a home and the promise of a better life. A fabulous life.

"I don't know why Monique chose my mother as most likely to follow in her glamorous footsteps."

"I would guess," Garek said softly, "that your mother was extraordinarily beautiful. Wasn't she?"

"Yes," Amy Louise Trent's extraordinarily beautiful daughter replied. "She was. But unlike Monique, who loved life, loved men, and loved herself most of all, my mother was uncertain, sad, afraid. She must have been abused as a child. She didn't like, much less love, herself, and was promiscuous despite her fear of men. And she was desperately addicted, an addiction of despair, to drugs. To heroin. She tried to kick her habit from time to time. Tried valiantly, fought hard, but inevitably failed. The decision to try again, to fight again, must have been terribly difficult for her. She was happy when she was high. *Only* when she was high. But still she fought. Still she tried."

"Did Monique understand how difficult it was for her?"

"Sometimes yes, sometimes no. Monique was like a parent, by turns proud, worried, frustrated, angry. My mother could have had the world. Monique had handed it to her more than once. But the liaisons never worked. The men always sent her back. Armande was her last chance. Monique's final offering. And her best. *The* best. Her own lover's eldest son. It was kismet, Monique decided, that the other relationships hadn't worked, because Armande's proper Parisian marriage had produced at last its proper number of sons, the heir and the spare. Armande would want my mother, as every man who saw her always did. And this time the balance would be tipped dramatically in favor of success. This time, for the first time, I'd be going, too."

"As your mother's keeper."

"Yes. Which I *wanted* to be. Armande's palazzo in Venice would also tip the balance. Venice would. The Bourbon Street prostitute who'd been mesmerized by the New World Mardi Gras would thrive in the year-round fairy tale that was Venice. At Monique's invitation, Armande flew to New Orleans to see my mother, to meet her."

"But when he saw you, met you . . ."

"No, Garek. We didn't see each other then. Didn't meet. And Armande definitely wanted my mother. We were scheduled to arrive in Venice at the perfect time. Carnivale. My mother seemed genuinely excited, authentically hopeful, courageously committed. This time, she vowed, she would win the battle against her addiction. She'd be on her way to triumph, she pledged, before we even departed New Orleans. But it was my mother who departed. The girl who'd run from her bayou home, her bayou horror, ran away again. She *would* have tried life without heroin in Venice, and with Armande and me. She would have fought that fight. But an opportunity presented itself she simply couldn't resist. A temptation. Money. Cash. Which she stole."

"Monique's money?"

"No. But she did steal from Monique, a brooch that had been a gift from Armande's father. Its sentimental value far exceeded its worth, and Monique viewed its theft as an ultimate, *the* ultimate, slap in her face. I tried to convince her that it was sentiment not malice that prompted my mother to take the brooch. She'd wanted a memory of Monique, a remembrance of her. For the same reason, I argued, she'd taken a sketch of Venice I was working on. But Monique was through giving Amy Louise Trent the benefit of any doubt. She wouldn't be happy, she raged, until the thieving addict was locked behind bars. Which *would* happen. The cops she'd bewitched over the years would, with a single call from her, launch a massive hunt for the fleeing ingrate. I pleaded with Monique not to make that call. I'd do anything. *Anything*."

"Including taking your mother's place as Armande's mistress."

They stood at water's edge, behind a wrought-iron water gate along a lamplit canal. The water wasn't quite glass, their reflections rippled slightly, a faint blurring, a gentle softening.

Giselle saw, in that liquid mirror, her own image . . . and her mother's.

"I didn't suggest it," she said to ripples of copper, of whiskey, of cream, the alluring sensuality both women shared. "It would never have occurred to me to do so. But it occurred to Monique right away. I was Gigi after all. Even though, in the seventeen years I'd lived in Monique's mansion academy, there'd never been the slightest indication that I was a mistress in training, too. It was, I suppose, simply understood."

"You were seventeen."

Giselle looked at the reflection beside hers. The rich brown hair, the dark blue eyes, the sorcery of gentleness and strength. Garek's image didn't ripple, even as hers did. Didn't drift, didn't tremble, didn't blur.

"Yes," she said.

"Innocent."

"Yes. And astonishingly naive. But none of that mattered."

"Compared to saving your mother's life."

"Compared to giving her the chance to save it."

"Did she?"

"I don't know. I never saw her again. Never heard from her. Or of her. I thought she'd come to Venice when she'd lost her fight with opiates—again. She'd reach out to Monique, and all would be forgiven, and when she learned that I was with Armande and she wouldn't have to be . . . I didn't *want* her to fail, of course."

"But you hoped she'd come to Venice."

"I really did. She would have loved it here. Been better here. Happy here."

"Were you happy here, Giselle? With Armande?"

Something touched the water then. A gust of winter, the wake of a bird, the sigh and swell of the Adriatic Sea. Giselle didn't know what caused the wave on their shimmering mirror, only that the sudden distortion caused her to look from the whimsical reflector to one that was true, constant, and brilliantly clear.

She saw herself in his glittering blue eyes. Armande's mistress. Aimee's loyal daughter. And, most of all, a woman whose happiness, it seemed, mattered to him. Garek. Very much.

"Happy with Armande? No. But happy in Venice? Yes. Finally. Once I released myself from my self-imposed prison behind the palazzo walls."

"You weren't happy with Armande," Garek affirmed quietly. "Yet if it was only nine years ago that you parted, you must have been with him, stayed with him, for almost eleven."

"For exactly eleven. From that first Carnivale, when I was seventeen, until my last—before this one—when I was twenty-eight. Ten of those eleven years were for my mother, to repay her debt. The stolen money had been replaced by Monique. But every penny needed to be reimbursed. By me. If I failed, Monique promised, she'd make her threatened call to the New Orleans police. I knew nothing of statutes of limitations in those days. Part of my naïveté. And even more naively, as it turns out, I trusted Monique. She'd receive annual payments from Armande, she told me. Her commission for arranging his liaison with me. It would take ten years, she said, for my mother's debt to be fully repaid."

"It must have been a great deal of money she'd stolen."

"To me, yes, and to my mother. But quite trivial to Monique. I didn't know that then, of course. How trivial it was to her. Nor did I know I could have repaid it all myself at the end of just one year. I needed to be with Armande, I believed, and to make him *want* me with him, for ten years."

"Which is what you did."

Giselle looked from blue mirror to churning water to a shadowy gargoyle on a roof nearby.

"It was all right," she told the ornamental gutter. "Once I discovered the glass factories of Murano, and the wonders of Venice itself. All right, being with Armande, for the first five years."

"And then?"

"And then," she whispered to the grotesque carving overhead, "he brought his fourteen-year-old son to the palazzo. To me. It was *tradition*, Armande told me. A gift bestowed by fathers' mistresses to their lovers' virgin sons. Armande's own first sexual experience at age twelve had been with Monique."

"He raped you."

The voice behind her was fierce, low, tender. And it didn't matter that she was looking away. The all-seeing eyes saw her still.

"No, Garek," she said as she turned. "I was never raped."

"You were, Giselle. From the start. By Monique, who made you believe you had no choice, and then by Armande."

"I believed I'd made a choice. I *had* made a choice. I'm not sure why I'm even telling you this. It's past history. *Ancient* history. Dead and buried."

Drowned, she thought, in a sea as deep, as blue, as his deep blue eyes. Except that nothing was that dark, that brilliant, that dangerous, that drowning. That blue.

"You're telling me," Garek McIntyre said softly, "because I want to know. All of it."

"It doesn't get better."

A faint smile touched his lips. "I had a feeling it didn't. Tell me."

"Two years later Armande brought his other son to me. He was just thirteen. But it was . . . easier anyway. Everything was easier by then. I'd been with Armande for seven years. Only three more to go. I could do it, I told myself. I could do *anything*."

"Including more rape."

"More proof of Armande's need to control me. And to

138

control anyone else, everyone else, that he possibly could. I was desirable to his friends, *desired* by them because of how I looked, so much like my mother, and because I belonged to Armande. He gave me grandly yet sparingly. Like all his possessions, my value enhanced the more rare I became. But there were select men, selected men, to whom he gave me for an hour, a weekend, a morning, a night. That was tradition, too, Armande claimed. The doge's courtesan coveted by all but shared with only a chosen few."

"There's another tradition," Garek said. "A better one. The fabled Venetian dagger. I imagine we could find some serviceable version, and you could point me in the direction of Armande's palazzo, and that would be that."

Garek spoke calmly, casually, of the legendary weapon of death. The dagger's long thin blade, once plunged to the hilt, came off with a twist, leaving massive hemorrhage within the victim and scarcely a telltale puncture without.

What would have been Giselle's light reply—You would never do such a thing!—was pierced by the ice-cold danger in his calm blue eyes.

"He isn't worth it," she said. "Besides, Armande's accomplice was as guilty as he."

"Monique."

"No, Garek, me. *Me.* I stayed with Armande, chose to, for that eleventh year. I stayed for me, not for my mother. Her debt was paid. But I needed money. I had none. Not a lira. Venice is a small city, and Armande envisioned himself to be its modern—if absentee and Parisian—doge. He was known, liked, revered. I was known, too, recognized everywhere. My signature was the only currency I ever needed.

139

Armande gave me neither money nor gifts. The gowns I wore belonged to him, as did the jewels. *I* belonged to him. I needed money to get away, to begin my new life. I knew how to make money. Gigi knew. I wanted to be paid, I told him, for sex with his friends. He could pay me, or they could. It didn't matter. It was a risk. Armande might have thrown me out to walk the streets. To *work* them."

"You would never have done that."

"But that's exactly what I *did* do, Garek, in suites not streets. I was a prostitute. There are worse words, but none that are better. Armande loved the idea, the power it gave him, the supreme control. He would decide who would have me, for how much, for how long, and when. It would be the 'clients,' however, who paid—and who, because they were paying, felt they could demand more from me, of me, than when I'd been a gift. *I didn't care. I would* be free. It was simply a matter of time."

"Another year." *Of rape.*

"It took that long. Because Armande was in control. He didn't know why I wanted the money, or how desperate I was. I had to pretend it was just a game to me, a way to add interest to the boredom of sex with his friends. Perversely, it made Armande want me more than ever, and to become even less willing to share. Still, by the end of that Carnivale I'd have enough. I'd already purchased a ticket to San Francisco, and was booked on the first flight out on Ash Wednesday. But on the eve of my departure, this Shrove Tuesday night nine years ago, Armande revealed the arrangements he'd made for me, and two of his friends, while *he* watched. I told him no, and revealed my own plans to leave him, leave Venice, the following day. He was stunned, enraged. Until comprehension dawned."

"You said you could have repaid your mother's entire debt by the end of the first year."

"*Easily*. Despite her personal closeness to Armande, Monique had negotiated aggressively for my services, and, of course, for the commission she would receive. As was customary, at least in the liaisons Monique arranged, Armande sent the entire annual amount, her share and mine, to her. Hadn't I known? he gloated. How hopelessly *naive* for someone so *impure*. Armande couldn't wait to share the joke with Monique, and called her then and there. She was in New Orleans, celebrating her thirtieth Mardi Gras, as glamorous as ever and even more rich. She hadn't needed to impound the money that was mine. But she was going to keep it, she said. She deserved it, had *earned* it. She'd taken us in after all, my mother and me, and given us *everything*. Was I really planning to leave Armande? she wondered. If so, I was obviously as foolish—and ungrateful—as my mother. I left the palazzo while Armande and Monique were still savoring the joke. I hated them, hated Venice, and hated myself most of all. I took that loathing with me, lugged it around with me for nine years."

"But now it's gone."

"Now it's gone. I didn't even need to see Armande. It was about me, not him. Not him at all."

"I still find myself wanting to get hold of one of those daggers."

"You could never do that."

"The hell of it, Giselle, is that I could . . ."

ELEVEN

$\mathcal{G}$arek McIntyre was the unwanted consequence of an extramarital fling, a one-night indiscretion regretted by both partners even as they indulged. He was born only because his mother had no way of knowing until postnatal blood studies were performed whether the baby she carried was the result of an unfortunate infidelity or an abiding love.

Garek spent his boyhood commuting between two families, neither of which wanted the living symbol of the marital lapse.

"That must have been so difficult for you," Giselle said.

There were mists in the night air, veils and vapors that floated and flew.

"Not really," Garek replied. "It was all I knew. And I

enjoyed the independence it afforded me, the chance to rely on myself, challenge myself, survive on my own."

"On your own?"

"Just for one night, the first time. On impulse, on one of my commuting weekends, I got off the bus at an intermediate stop. I'd just spend a few hours exploring, I decided. But I ended up staying the night. I loved every minute of it. The challenge, the freedom."

"The danger?"

He smiled. "That too. It was a little dangerous. I was just a boy. An *un*missed boy I discovered the following day. The assumption had simply been made, without a phone call to confirm, that I wouldn't be coming for the weekend after all. I had carte blanche after that, as many solitary adventures as I liked, entire weekends on my own in unfamiliar places, the more strange, unsavory, intriguing the better. I liked the edge. The edginess. Thrived on it, the challenge, both physical and mental. How much thirst could I handle? How much hunger, how little sleep? Eventually, when I'd pushed myself as far as I could, I began wondering how far could others push me. How far I would *let* them push."

"Others?"

"I decided to let the Navy SEALs take their best shot. I was wrong for the SEALs, for any special forces unit for that matter. Not a team player in a setting where the team was all. But I made the cut for BUD/S, the boot camp, flipper camp, for SEAL hopefuls. I wasn't the only loner in that BUD/S class. There were seven of us. Arrogant all, quarterbacks all, unwilling to trust even insignificant decisions, much less life-and-death ones, to anyone else. They put the seven of us together in BUD/S, with the thought that we'd either force each other out in a hurry or become the SEALs team we became. We worked as that team for seven years. Seven men. Seven years."

"I've heard about the Navy SEALs," Giselle murmured to a drifting cloud of dew.

Garek had been Giselle's mirror when she'd told him of Gigi. He needed the same, now, from her, needed to see, as he revealed himself, his reflection in her eyes.

He waited in silence. Until, in silence, she looked from the drifting cloud to him.

"Everything you've heard is true, Giselle, and then some. With no apologies. SEALs are trained for combat. For war. They do the necessary jobs, the essential tasks, swiftly, thoroughly, professionally. Those jobs are dirty, sometimes. Ugly. But they are always necessary."

"And dangerous," she said, worried even as she shimmered. For him. Even as she glowed.

His smile was a little wicked, a little wry. "Sure. That goes with the territory. But with experience, as you get better at what you do and assuming you're paying attention, you can minimize the danger, control the risks, even as the jobs become more challenging."

"As they did for your team?"

"Yes. They did. We developed a specialty over time. Hostage rescue. It requires specialized training, not to mention a mindset that runs contrary to the usual warrior mandates of take no prisoners and search-and-destroy. We liked the added challenge, the enhanced danger, and we liked the results."

"The safely rescued hostages?"

"The safely rescued hostages," Garek confirmed. "Always a deliriously happy bunch." He drew a breath, inhaled sea vapors, and added softly, "It wasn't even a rescue mission that ravaged our team. Nothing that treacherous. Only two of the seven of us survived. John and I. The others were victims of a well-planned ambush, a massacre, courtesy of a squadron of snipers, and the faulty intelligence we'd received. We wanted to bring our five friends out, John and I. To bring them home. But we couldn't give them even that."

The mists were ghosts now, in the air, in his eyes, in his heart.

"I'm sorry."

"So was I, Giselle, and always will be. I was angry, too. Very. Not surprisingly, anger isn't a terribly useful emotion in a warrior, particularly when it's directed at your own side."

"You left the SEALs."

"And the Navy."

"And became a lawyer."

A spark of blue glinted amid the ghosts. "It was a new challenge."

"And, as an expert in contract law, you're specializing in rescue missions still."

"Am I?"

"Aren't you? By being on the lookout for the land mines that might be lurking in the fine print? And, by exploding said mines before permitting any signing on the dotted line, aren't you rescuing your clients in advance from a hostage situation that might result?"

She was so lovely, his copper-haired mirror. *So lovely.*

"Maybe," he said. "Maybe that is the appeal to me. The challenge to me. I know for a fact what enticed me to move from New York to Chicago. You."

You. It floated like joy in the lacy winter air.

"Me?"

"You." *You, you, you.* "And your snowflake chimes. I'd been with a firm in New York for a while. Not looking to move. But a Chicago firm made me an offer I really had to consider. They flew me in, and arranged a room for me at the Wind Chimes Hotel. I had an evening of being wined and dined ahead, so my first glance at your pastel snowfall was a fleeting one. But on my return, and all throughout the night, I stood beneath the chimes, looking at them, talking to them, listening to their various replies."

It was a remarkable image, the ex-SEAL consulting with a chime of glassy snowflakes, and a fanciful image, for he was, first and foremost, a man who relied on himself. And it was magical, too, the image—as magical as this Venetian night of mists and mirrors.

"You're thinking," Garek said softly, "that what I'm telling you isn't true. That, among other things, the chimes are silent, *silenced*, from midnight until six."

"They are."

"I heard them, Giselle. Throughout the night. They're very polite, your delicate snowflakes, but enthusiastic. When they approved of a decision I made, they fluttered

146

their applause. Move to Chicago? Yes. They liked that. And in solo practice, not with the firm? Very wise, they concurred. That team player thing. And there was, for such daintiness, an almost deafening flurry of chiming when I floated the proposition that I both work and live in the adjoining Towers, as if the sister snow chime in the lobby there had joined the ovation, too. Don't doubt this, Giselle. It happened."

She smiled, and nodded, believing everything on this night of magic and masquerade.

Believing him.

"Three weeks later I was in the Towers' condo I'd just purchased thinking about its decor. It was basically good, an understatement of color and style that didn't distract from the views of sky, of city, of lake. Even the mirrored walls managed to enhance, not detract. But I needed something in the living room, I decided. Something as spectacular as the vistas outside. A snow chime, I thought, or maybe another Giselle Trouveau work of art? What I found, what I bought, was *Venetian Dawn*."

"*Venetian Destiny*."

"*Destiny*?"

"My name for it. Never before spoken aloud."

"Because?"

"Because," she confessed, "I seem to be telling you everything."

"And I, you. I want to be."

"So do I."

"Then tell me, Giselle, why you called the piece *Destiny*."

"Because it was my first completed sculpture, the first in which what I'd envisioned, the golden splendor of a Venetian dawn, and what I'd been able to create were the same. I'd been dreaming for so long about being able to do just that. Dreaming, but not knowing until then that I really could. It felt like destiny when I finished it. It *was* destiny. The reason I'd lived in Venice all those years."

"I was told I was the first owner."

"You were. You are. *Dawn—Destiny*—had been keeping me company in my studio for quite some time. I thought I'd never sell it. Had no need to. Didn't want to. But one day it felt . . . necessary to sell it. *Right* to. It felt, that day, like destiny." Giselle looked at the man who controlled danger, managed risk, went one-on-one with fate and almost always won. "You're probably not a big believer in destiny. Even though," she added to what looked like wonder in the dangerous blue, "you believe in the polite applause of snowflakes."

"I saw you, Giselle."

You *see* me. "Saw me, Garek?"

"Here. In Venice. Twenty years ago."

"Oh," she whispered with wonder, and seeing too. Seeing *too*. "And I saw you."

"You couldn't have. I would have been invisible to you."

"Yes, but . . . it was December 8. And it was snowing."

"Pastel snowflakes."

"They caught, in their tiny prisms of ice, the softest hues of the winter light. The lavenders, the aquas, the pinks."

"Your hair was long. To your waist. Burnished fire. You

stood on a bridge, gazing heavenward, smiling as the flakes fell on your face."

"I thought the angels were having a pillow fight. A pillow party. To which I'd been invited. I'd been so lonely in Venice. So lonely all my life." *Until that snow-in-Venice day.* "There was a *pensione* across the canal. You were on the second floor, standing at the corner window."

"You looked right at me. But you couldn't possibly have seen into the shadows."

"No. I couldn't see. But I wanted to. I *tried* to."

"Until you remembered Armande. I saw so clearly when you did, your confusion, your worry, your alarm."

"I ran away then. Ran away, like my mother."

"You were running toward promises you'd made, Giselle. Not away. I saw that, too. I saw *so clearly* that you weren't free. I almost ran after you anyway. To hell with your promises, and with mine. I was due back in Florence that evening. We'd had a few days off, a little necessary R and R. I'd come to Venice alone and was running late when I saw you. I'd lingered on a vaporetto too long on Murano, a lingering made even longer by the leisurely snow schedule the boats were on."

"How long have you known?"

"That you were the girl on the bridge? Just this evening. Just now. I came to Venice to meet the reclusive artist and see her work. I've never even seen a photograph of you. As far as I can tell there aren't any. I had to be in Geneva, and your gallery had sent me a notice that you'd be here, and . . . if I'd known it was you, who you were, who you are, I wouldn't have come. Shouldn't have come."

For it was he, on this February night, who had commitments to honor. Promises to keep.

To his wife. She was here, a floating mist, with him. With them. And she needed, before it was too late, to be formally introduced.

"Her name," Garek said, "is Kathleen. We met in Chicago shortly after my move. She both lived and worked in the Towers, too. Her position at station WCHM, which broadcasts from the building's ninth and tenth floors, was as a radio talk-show host. She'd been offered TV. Keeps being offered it. But she prefers a forum in which her words, her intelligence, are all that count. Her audience is huge, and as diverse as the topics she handles with ease, from relationships to politics to the Bulls and the Bears—both kinds, the sports teams in Chicago and wizards of Wall Street in New York."

"You're very proud of her."

"Very. I also respect her, and care about her. But I'm not in love with her, Giselle. *We're* not in love. Nor have we ever been. We both knew it, talked about it, *liked* it. What we had felt more stable to us, a compatibility that was in all regards a perfect fit. We considered living together, discussed it at length. Since we didn't anticipate having children, that reason for marriage—a primary one, we both agreed—didn't exist. But we also had every intention of spending our lives together, faithfully, happily, for better or worse. We chose to acknowledge that promise, to celebrate it, in the traditional way."

"But something happened."

"The happily part. Kathleen hasn't been happy for a

while. I don't know why. She doesn't know why. At least she didn't know when we separated four months ago. It was her suggestion to separate, and of course I agreed. She needed to find out what was wrong, what had changed. Was it me? Was it her? Was it us? The future, I told her, *our* future was entirely her call. If she wanted out of the marriage, if it was best for her, happier for her, then so be it. But if we could make it work, and she wanted that still, I'd be there."

"Have you heard from her?"

"She called two days ago. She sounded good. Terrific, actually. The old Kathleen. Confident and strong. She'd wanted that Kathleen back. We both had. She, that old Kathleen, is ready for us to talk."

"But not to say good-bye."

"I don't think so. No."

They weren't touching, Garek and Giselle. Had not touched. Even the mists from their breaths, that warmth in the cool winter air, didn't touch, didn't mingle, did not, even high in the sky, become one.

They were that far apart.

And so very close.

"There's something else, isn't there?" she asked.

"You mean other than you? Other than destiny? Don't tell me you're not feeling it, Giselle. Feeling *us*."

"I won't. I can't. Of course I am. But we've only known each other for six hours, and this is Venice, this fairy tale, and . . . I can't tell you I'm not feeling it, Garek. I would never tell you that."

151

"We've known each other for six hours," he said softly, "and twenty years. Haven't we?"

"Yes," she whispered. *Yes.*

"I could tell Kathleen that I, too, have changed. And that I'd be as unhappy in the marriage now as she'd been when we decided to separate. I could even tell her about you, Giselle. Every truth. All six hours and twenty years. She'd be amazed but accepting. She'd wish me, wish us, the best. I *will* tell her the truth. Unless," he said quietly, "what she tells me first, the reason she sounds like the old Kathleen and more—something radiant and glowing and new—is that she's four months pregnant with my child."

He'd commuted between two homes as a boy, unwanted by each. And he'd challenged himself to survive, as he must, on his own.

Garek McIntyre was magnificent proof that a neglected child need not become a neglectful and negligent man. He'd survived brilliantly. Honorably.

But this man, this father, would not wish such loneliness, such aloneness, on any child. Much less his own.

"Kathleen never needs to know about me, Garek. Never. You've done nothing she ever needs to know. You haven't even touched me."

"I don't dare touch you, Giselle. If I did, I'd never let you go. And, if Kathleen's pregnant, I must. I *will*." It was a promise, harsh and soft and low. Then more softly, and still harsh and low, he made its mirror-image vow. "But if she's not pregnant, you will hear from me. Soon. If it's our destiny to be together, Giselle, you will hear."

TWELVE

$\mathcal{G}$iselle never heard from the man she loved. But Garek was with her, watching her proudly, lovingly, as she spun, as she twirled, as she reached for the moon.

And did her invisible skater inspire from afar her creations of glass? Of course he did. As he had from the very start, that snowy day in Venice.

Giselle had been blind until that day of snowflakes on gondolas, and winged lions, and mosaics of gold. She'd lived in darkness until that day, in blackness, imprisoned in Armande's palazzo—she'd imprisoned herself—hoping he wouldn't come, feeling more trapped when he did, and waiting for her mother, not wanting her to have failed, but so lonely. So alone.

She'd been a fragile wisteria, that delicate bloom of a city with no gardens, clinging to whatever she could, not knowing where to blossom and so fearful she would drown.

Until that December day. That Garek McIntyre day. Alone no more. Lonely no longer. The brightness had lingered even after he was gone. She'd journeyed to Murano, where Garek had lingered in the snow, and had found her destiny of flames and glass.

A message from Pierce had greeted Giselle on her return from the Festival of Masks. He wanted her to view by helicopter an island he'd purchased—in the event, even in advance of his architectural drawings, she had thoughts.

And oh, had Giselle had thoughts about the snowy moonscape she saw.

It was La Serenissima, nestled amid mountains a mile above the sea. Giselle adorned with glass Pierce's most serene island in the Rockies. With glass, with joy, with love.

Because of Garek.

And now the man who'd made—and kept—his promises to his wife, to his child, *and to her*, had made promises as well to Grace Alysia Quinn. To find her. To rescue her.

And, now, with Giselle's help, Garek would keep those solemn vows.

Giselle knew exactly where the snapshots were. Not that she needed them. She was so very sure.

She booked a morning flight to Chicago and reserved a room at the Wind Chimes Hotel. She heard her chiming snowflakes as she made the reservation, although her name, it seemed, rang not a bell. Which was good. Fine. Easiest. Best.

Or maybe the Wind Chimes clerk was merely focused, as all of Chicago apparently was, on a different flurry of snow. A *fury* if the forecasters were right. Which, the clerk said, everyone believed they were.

Chicago was on the verge of its heaviest snowfall in memory. It was coming from Canada, a steady as she goes—steady as she snows—pace that enabled remarkable specificity about when the first Windy City flakes would fall. Six o'clock tomorrow evening. At the height of the Friday commute.

This was going to be a serious storm, and everyone was taking it seriously. City workers, all save emergency personnel, would be sent home early, and private-sector employers were encouraged to follow suit.

Surrender, both newscasters and forecasters advised, to being snowed in for the weekend. Get yourself where you want to be and *enjoy* it. For three days, if possible.

Yes, the main lines would likely be passable by Monday, and O'Hare would undoubtedly have re-opened. But if you didn't *have* to be anywhere until Tuesday, if you could enjoy the winter wonderland until then, by all means *do* so.

Giselle reserved her hotel room through Monday and, at the clerk's recommendation, because the Friday afternoon cab lines at the airport could be "amazing," arranged to be met at O'Hare by a hotel limousine.

Then, save for finding the photos and packing for snow, she was ready for her trip to Chicago. To Garek. And it was time to call, time to relinquish her guardianship of the truth about Grace, a custody she'd never even known she had.

It was 9:11 Carmel time—11:11 P.M. in Chicago.

The late-night call was greeted by a recorded voice. A

155

woman's voice. Smiling, welcoming, encouraging. A radio voice. *Kathleen's*. The loner and his lover were searching together. Rescuing together.

Loner and lover. Father and mother.

Husband and wife.

At the sound of the beep, Giselle provided her name and number. Then, "I know who Grace is. I met her in New Orleans twenty-three years ago. She was with me from January eighteenth until the twenty-fourth. After that, until her high-school graduation ten years later, she lived in an orphanage."

Giselle spoke—and spelled—the name by which she'd known Grace, and the name, address, and phone number of the orphanage where Grace had lived. Grace would have no insight into her true identity, Giselle asserted, and what she believed to be true would be a monstrous lie.

Giselle disclosed the lie crafted by the monster himself, Troy Logan, as well as the fact of the two snapshots she had. "I'll bring the photos with me tomorrow. Assuming my flight's on time and the snowstorm's not early, I should be in my room at the Wind Chimes a little after noon. I'll call when I arrive."

Giselle said nothing about her acquaintance—acquaintance?—with Garek. Nor, beyond her name, did she identify herself.

Whoever was assigned to listen to the overnight phone calls would, come morning, advise Garek about a message as definitive as hers.

I know who Grace is. I have photographs of Grace.

Giselle had just started packing when her telephone rang.

"Giselle," he greeted softly.

So softly. "Garek."

"Hi."

"Hi."

"I was awake, listening to calls, and there you were."

I was in Venice, he thought, looking out my window, and there you were. And in Venice again, to see a collection of masks, and there you were.

I was in darkness, she thought, until the brightness of snow, and there you were. And in darkness again, until my return to Venice, and there you were.

And here you are, she thought in the gentle silence. Again. To rescue from darkness a lost little girl.

"I know who she is, Garek. I'm so *certain* that I do."

"I believe you," he said. "And I believe that you do. With the information you've provided, we should be able to find her quickly, easily. Tomorrow."

"I hope so. She needs to know the truth. Soon. Thanks to me, she's been living a lie."

"Not thanks to you, Giselle. Thanks to Troy."

"But I repeated it. *Reinforced* it."

"In good faith."

Good faith, Giselle mused. Like a promise. Like Garek's promises, soft and low, to her. If Kathleen wasn't pregnant, he'd promised, she would hear from him. Soon. And if Kathleen *was* carrying his child? Giselle would never hear from him again. Ever.

Those were the promises, the necessary rules. And now, as if the rules had magically changed, Giselle had made plans to see him.

But nothing had changed. *Their* destiny, Giselle's and Garek's, hadn't. Only Grace's had.

Grace Alysia Quinn was destined to be found. Rescued. Saved. And as for the photos Giselle had? The tangible proof that her story was true?

Garek didn't doubt her story. Didn't doubt *her*. No proof was required.

And neither was she.

"Would it be better if I didn't come to Chicago, Garek? Best? Would you rather not see me?"

I would give my life to see you. "I can't see you, Giselle."

She heard the emotion in his voice. Hoarse, harsh, aching, raw. He wanted to see her. But couldn't. Could not. For all of them. His wife. His child. Giselle. Himself.

"I understand. I shouldn't have—"

"You don't understand, Giselle. I can't see you. Literally. I'm just a little too blind."

"Blind, Garek?" *Blind Garek?* "But when? How? *Why?*"

"I have no idea why." *Destiny, maybe? Punishment?* "But as to when, at dawn the morning after I left Venice." *Left you.* "And as to how, I didn't tell you in Venice what became of the other survivor of our SEAL team."

"John."

"Yes. John. He left the Navy, as I did, but subsequently returned. As, Giselle, did I. Not quite as formally as John, nor as officially."

"But you did more . . . jobs?"

"Rescue missions only. And only when I had something specific to contribute."

"Like your experience. Your expertise. That's why you were in Geneva."

"That was our staging area. The hostages were in the Balkans."

"You didn't tell me."

"I knew you'd worry, and I didn't want you to. There wasn't any *need* to worry. The rescue mission was easy. Straightforward. The hostages had been held for less than a week. Their captors weren't expecting a rescue effort anytime soon. But because those captors were also novices at terror, unpredictable and undisciplined, an early rescue was essential. There was reason to be concerned that in their inexperience, and their zealousness, they were quite capable of executing their captives on the purest whim. There weren't any surprises awaiting us. It *was* easy. They *weren't* expecting us. But as if I were the novice, I was careless. The good news is that only I was injured."

"*Good news?*"

"Carelessness is bad enough. Inexcusable. But when you risk lives other than your own, the inexcusable becomes the unforgivable. I deserved what I got. I'm just grateful I didn't take anyone else with me."

"But *Garek*."

She heard a soft laugh, and when he spoke again she heard his smile. "I'm okay, Giselle. Not thrilled, admittedly, but managing. Adapting. And forever indebted to the software geniuses who've made it possible to hear the typewritten word. It turns out I can still practice contract law."

"And lead rescue missions."

"Hardly. Although I consult with John from time to time."

"I meant the rescue mission for Grace."

"Ah. Well. That's a personal thank-you to Jace Colton, the teenage runaway Grace knew as Sam. Jace is a trauma surgeon these days, and fortunately for me was in the Balkans, volunteering at a hospital, at the time. He couldn't do anything about my blindness, no one could have, but there were other injuries. Life-threatening ones."

"He saved your life."

"Yes, he did."

"And now you're finding Grace, saving Grace, for him."

"And for her. For everyone, for that matter, who loved her. No one expects her to remember them. But they want her to know who she was, and how much she was loved."

"I want that, too."

"And to be here when word comes that she's been found?"

Was he asking if she wanted to travel to Chicago still? Now that she knew he was blind? As if such darkness might possibly make a difference to her?

"I'd like that very much."

She heard silence. Silence. As black as night and dagger-sharp.

Then soft, as soft, as snow.

"Then come, Giselle, as you've planned. In the morning before the storm. I won't be able to . . . see you, however, until seven-thirty tomorrow night. I have a prior commitment away from the office for the entire day. And even tomorrow night, I'm afraid, we can only meet until nine."

"That's *fine*, Garek. I understand. You have commitments"—*promises*—"to your child. Your children? I really . . . maybe this isn't such a good idea."

160

"I have no child, Giselle. No children. Kathleen wasn't pregnant after all."

"But the two of you are still married."

"No. We're not."

"Oh." *I see, and you don't, and what about the promises, Garek, that you made to me?*

THIRTEEN

*T*he voice on the Finding Grace hot line belonged to Garek's secretary, Olympia.

"Hello, hello!" the voice greeted on the taped message that awaited Giselle's arrival in her lakeview suite, a complimentary upgrade, the artist recognized after all. "And *welcome*. Once you're settled, please give me a call and I'll pop right on over."

Giselle returned Olympia's call immediately. She wasn't settled. Far from it. But this time, she knew, her serenity had nothing to do with baggage.

Besides, it was after three. Her flight had departed—and landed—two hours late, thanks to air-traffic gridlock at SFO.

"I'd be happy to pop right on over to you."

"I may be old, dear, but I *am* ambulatory. And Garek wants me to show you how to get from where you are to where he is, will be, at seven-thirty tonight."

Olympia appeared in nine minutes. She was far from old, merely in her seventies, and as lively as her voice, and indeed most ambulatory. She moved at a brisk clip, talking as she did, and stopping abruptly, not to rest but to admire, when they reached the lobby of the hotel.

Giselle's snowflakes chimed overhead, and above the rainbowed flutter a domed skylight revealed a pure white sky.

"It doesn't look very ominous, does it?" Olympia asked. "But as a Chicago native, I can tell you this is the proverbial calm before the storm. Said storm is the reason I'm escorting you. It's unclear whether the Towers' evening-shift doorman will be coming in. He *shouldn't*. But he's a show-must-go-on sort of fellow. However, in the event that reason prevails and he stays home, you'll need to know how to open the locked doors you'll encounter between here and there. Garek would come get you, of course, but . . ."

"He told me about his blindness."

"*That* wouldn't stop him, and his politeness—well. The point is he can't walk this far, Giselle. He mustn't. Not tonight."

Olympia's mysterious pronouncement remained unexplained. They'd reached the first of the potentially locked doors.

Giselle entered on the touch pad the numbers Olympia had written down for her and was rewarded with a gratifying *click*. She repeated the process five minutes later, at the Towers end of the enclosed walkway, with different numbers but identical success.

The Towers' day-shift doorman wandered over to see what Olympia was up to, and when introduced to Olympia's companion began a heartfelt rave. Thanks to Giselle's chimes, he said, he loved coming to work. *Loved* it.

Garek lived on the Towers' top floor. Ascent, absent the doorman, was accomplished by entering a third set of numbers onto a panel within the elevator itself.

Garek's penthouse was unlocked the old-fashioned way, not by code but by key, one of which jangled on Olympia's key ring.

"Garek wanted me to check—oh, good," Olympia observed as she opened the door to the recently vacuumed, hence footprint-free, carpet. "Housekeeping's been here, as promised. Come *in*, Giselle."

It was magnificent, this place where Garek lived, and where she and Olympia left shoeless prints he would never see.

Magnificent. And so solitary.

Giselle felt the solitude at once. The loner was relying on himself, challenging himself, surviving brilliantly. Again. Alone.

Choosing to.

His penthouse was, as he'd described, an understatement of color and style, its splendor drawn from the views he could not see, and brought inside, as he'd told her, by the walls of mirrors.

And, as he'd told her, in the living room was *Venetian Dawn*.

Venetian Destiny.

It glowed gold, her sculpture of graceful swirls and shimmering glass, as if oblivious to the blackness of the world in which Garek McIntyre dwelled. Or maybe *Destiny* was smiling at Olympia, who was smiling in reply, as the sculpture had smiled for so many years at Giselle.

"Do you know what happened, Olympia, that morning in the Balkans?" *That golden dawn that was Garek's night-black destiny?* "It was a military operation, Garek said, a hostage rescue."

Olympia's smile disappeared. "Yes. It was. And I do know. Not from Garek, mind you. By the time he was stable enough to be transported back to Chicago his focus was where it had to be, on the present not the past. But he had visitors, men who'd been with him on that fateful day. He was shot, Giselle, at point-blank range. And as if a barrage of bullets wasn't enough, he fell backwards onto a rock. A boulder, I suppose. He hit his head, his skull, the occipital lobes of his brain. *Both* occipital lobes at the place where they almost touch. That's why his loss of vision is total. Just a *millimeter* to either side and he would have been able to see half a world."

"I don't understand. If it was a military operation, Garek would have been wearing a bulletproof vest. Don't they always? And some sort of combat helmet, too?"

"That's precisely what I said when I heard the news. It simply could not have happened. No way, *so there*! But it did happen, Giselle. Garek and the others had gone in believing there were only four hostages. For whom, by the way, they had helmets and vests. But there was a fifth hostage. A teenage girl. She was more prisoner than hostage, if such a distinction can be made, a native of the embattled region who'd been captured by enemy soldiers for pleasure, not for ransom."

"She'd been raped?"

"Repeatedly. The American hostages had no idea she was even there. She'd been too proud to scream. Or too frightened. Or too battered. By the time she was thrown in with the other hostages, she was delirious, dying, *going* to die. It was obvious, apparently, that her situation was hopeless. And Garek had been trained to know what to do."

"To put her out of her misery, Olympia? Is that what you mean?"

"What? *No.* Well, I *don't* know. But I can't imagine Garek would ever—I don't *want* to imagine it. No one mentioned *that*, only that he should have known, certainly did know, to leave her behind. Which amounts to the same thing, I guess, doesn't it? Condemning her to death?"

"Which he didn't do. Couldn't do. He's a rescuer."

"I've never thought of him quite that way. But," Olympia said, "it's the *right* way. Garek is, most definitely, a rescuer. As he was on that day. He gave the girl *his* helmet, *his* vest, put them on her scarcely conscious body himself, then carried her to where a helicopter was waiting to fly them to safety. It was a flawless rescue, a flawless escape, until she opened her eyes and in her delirium saw her

166

most fearsome enemy—a man. She shot him with his own gun and died without ever knowing she'd done so."

"She was shot, too? By someone else on the team?"

"No. Both she and Garek were airlifted to the nearest medical facility. Which wasn't much, except for its personnel."

"Trauma surgeon Jace Colton. Garek did tell me that."

"Jace did everything humanly possible to save the girl. He would have done so no matter what Garek, or anyone, wanted him to do. But Garek wanted her to live. Desperately. As much, maybe more, than he himself wanted to survive. He was similarly insistent that she never be told what she'd done. She never regained consciousness enough to be told. She died, as she was *destined* to die before her rescuer ever arrived, and he, that rescuer, spent the next six months in and out of the hospital—mostly in—recovering from the many things a point-blank arsenal of bullets can do. He recovered completely, remarkably, from all but the brutal assault of the rock. How fair is that?"

"Not fair at all, Olympia." I was careless, Garek had told her. I deserved what I got. *Careless, Garek?* For caring so much, too much, about a dying girl who'd been repeatedly raped? "He's very lucky to have you."

"No, dear, *I'm* lucky to have *him*. In fact, I'm another Garek McIntyre rescuee. I'd been at my previous job for forty-seven years. My only credentials when I started were the ability to type, to file, to spell. Over time, in addition to familiarizing myself with the technological advances that came along, I'd learned a thing or two about the law. If I *do* say so myself. Garek was being aggressively recruited to join our firm. He was a rainmaker—the legal equivalent, I guess you could say, of a rescuer. His visit coincided with my sixty-fifth birthday. By week's end I'd be unemployed. Mandatorily retired. My original boss was enjoying his golden years in sunny Florida, and a younger generation was running the show. I wasn't ready to retire, or *old* enough to. It wasn't that I was particularly worried about filling my time. Although I suspect my daughters were. All three were single then, and not eager for the kind of motherly supervision I might have offered had I been available full-time."

"I bet they weren't that worried."

"No." Her smile revealed the closeness she shared with her girls. "And *yes*. But more to the point, I really enjoyed the work I was doing, enjoyed being good at it, and my husband, an accountant with his own business, was going strong at sixty-eight. So there I was, with my birthday balloons and farewell cake, when Garek appeared. I thought I was being perfectly chipper, professional to the core, but when Garek observed that I seemed a bit morose for a birthday girl, I confessed all. The following morning, when Garek returned to report his decision to go into solo practice in lieu of joining the firm, he offered me a job. That was nine years ago. We've had a few conversations, all prompted by him, about giving me a title *other* than secretary. Something more modern, more politically correct, and, of course, commensurate with the ridiculously enormous salary he keeps sending my way."

"Commensurate, Olympia, with what you do."

"So he says. Anyway, I'm a secretary and proud of it.

I'm also a grandmother these days, if you can believe it. *Three* times over."

"So you may be thinking about retiring?"

"Actually, Garek brought it up in early August, thinking I might be thinking about it. I hadn't been, but there were those grandbabies. He'd been thinking about taking some time off himself, he said. We'd spend the rest of the summer, we decided, wrapping things up, enough so that he'd feel comfortable leaving the office for a while, and that I'd feel comfortable leaving him. Literally the next day, however, we got word about Grace, that she was still alive. We were both immediately involved, wanted to be, and committed, both of us, to seeing it through. Which," she murmured, "as of today we just may have."

"If you're thinking Garek doesn't need you, Olympia . . ."

"I know that he does, Giselle. And that he *doesn't*. But I will miss him."

"As he'll miss you, for all the reasons you'll miss him, and then some. You're his eyes."

"No, dear. Garek is his own eyes. Except," she clarified with a twinkle, "when it comes to analyzing photographs. Shall we? I have one to show you, too. Her graduation from high school. But let's see yours first."

Giselle retrieved the two-frame photo strip from her purse and handed it to Olympia, who predictably frowned.

"Poor little thing. It's a far cry, isn't it, from the way she looked just a month before? She looks so old for such a little girl. And wise. In a world-weary way. No wonder the orphanage administrators decided she was eight."

"If you focus on the features one by one, Olympia, I

think you'll see . . ." Giselle didn't need to complete her sentence. Olympia was nodding. Seeing. "And almost as significant is the way these photos came to be. We were shopping for her trip the following day. When she spotted the photo booth, her hand tightened in mine and she tugged me toward it. She'd been so bewildered until then. Lost. Dazed. But suddenly, and eloquently despite her silence, she became focused. Determined. She wanted photos of the two of us together. She even smiled for them. Yes, that *is* a smile. After the fourth flash, she knew our turn was over. She led me to where the developed film would appear and collected two plastic sheaths from an adjacent slot. When the four-frame strip was ready, she creased it, tore it, placed each half in a sheath, and gave the top one to me."

"Just as she gave the top to Dinah."

"And as with Dinah," Giselle said, "the crease wasn't quite square. The resulting tear in both instances is angled from left to right. *Identically*, I think."

"I think so, too. What happened then?"

"Nothing. The burst of energy, the clarity of purpose, were gone as suddenly as they'd appeared. She was aware of the photographs she held, but was confused by them, as if she'd been following a posthypnotic suggestion she couldn't remember but was obliged to obey."

"She was following a memory."

"I think so. Yes."

"May I have these for a while?"

"Of course."

"Did Grace take her half with her?"

"Yes. But even if she has it still, it would prove only that she was the girl I met in New Orleans, not that she was Grace. Except that you just called her Grace."

"I did. She is."

Olympia revealed her photograph. It was taken in black-and-white, as high-school portraits often were.

The face was serious, beautiful.

And it was Giselle's turn to frown.

"I couldn't tell you with any certainty that this is the sixteen-year-old version of the girl I knew at six. And she doesn't look like either of her parents. Does she?"

"No. At least not to me. When this appeared on my computer screen, I felt that despite your certainty, you must be mistaken. Still, I did with it what I do with every photograph we receive. I forwarded it electronically to Carolyn Logan."

"Troy's widow?"

"Yes. The villainess of the piece. An undeserving title in my estimation. Carolyn was not the only one who believed Troy's lies. And Carolyn has been as committed as everyone else to finding Grace. True, her motivation may derive from guilt, not love. She'd hadn't the slightest desire to raise Mary Beth's orphaned daughter as her own. That selfishness, I believe she knows, made her far less questioning of Troy's plans for Grace than she should have been. Her guilt, as motivating as it might be, would enable her to be more objective, I decided. More detached. Besides, Carolyn Logan is geographically detached these days, living in Palm Springs not Loganville, so no one drops by her Splendor Mountain mansion to find out if there's been any word. We told Grace's loved ones that we wouldn't be telling them anything, no matter how promising a lead might seem, until we *knew* we'd found her. And that Grace knew it, too. We hadn't planned to have anyone screen photos, on the grounds we'd be investigating all leads anyway, but Carolyn wanted to do something. Anything. So when I received the first of so many photographs that looked to me *exactly* like Mary Beth, I beamed it from my computer to hers. No way, Carolyn said. No resemblance to the real Mary Beth Quinn at all."

"You've had many such photos? In just one week?"

"Amazing, isn't it? And they've *all* been legit. Women who honestly believe they might be Grace. Our investigators check every one, even when Carolyn says they needn't bother."

"Carolyn thought this high-school photo looked like Mary Beth?"

"She said it *was* Mary Beth. The tilt of the head, the cast of the eyes, the expression itself. She'd known Mary Beth well. They were high-school rivals for Troy. Carolyn's not that detached, by the way. She was breathless when she called. Elated. I'm eager to hear what she thinks of your photos. She *knows* how Grace looked after the fire. She saw her every day for the three weeks Grace was hidden in Troy's Loganville home."

"You need to send the photos to her soon, Olympia, so you can go home, be home, before it starts to snow."

"You sound just like Garek! Don't worry, I will." Olympia cast an informed glance at the twilight sky. "It's still at least ninety minutes away. And that's just the first

172

snowflake. But I'll definitely be on my way before then. Carolyn's on standby. She'll give me about a one-minute turnaround time, and once the investigators get back to me, I'll give Garek the final update—which, the investigators have promised, will include where Grace is living now. I'll let Garek tell you that, if you don't mind. Let him have at least some part of this monumental day. After all the work he's put into this search to have missed this day of all days. Not that he *resents* it. Finding Grace is all that matters. But *still*."

"He said he had a prior commitment away from the office."

"Commitment? Yes, I suppose at this point that's all it is. Six months ago I'd have described it as a rendezvous, that more romantic term, even though then as now his assignation was with an arteriogram."

"An arteriogram?"

"A *cerebral* one. And, I'm afraid, it's even *worse* than it sounds. The arteriogram part is fairly standard, tiny catheters threaded into blood vessels in the brain. But what's being infused through those catheters is far from standard, and there's nothing remotely routine in the discomfort, the *pain*, the infusion provokes. My source, as you might imagine, is *not* Garek. He acts like it's no big deal. But it is. Very big."

"Today isn't his first time."

"No. It's his *sixth*. And last. He's had one every thirty days, no matter the day of the week, for the past six months. He's seeing the entire extravaganza through to the bitter end, in the event it might benefit someone else, even though it hasn't helped him."

"But it might have helped him, Olympia? Might have helped his blindness?"

"*Yes*. It seemed so promising six months ago. He was *so* hopeful. He tried to hide it. To be 'cautiously optimistic' as the medical folks like to say. But hope was there. Quiet. Powerful. And *reasonable*. He'd begun seeing lights, you see. *Lights* where there'd been only darkness. I don't know if you've kept up on the heart-attack literature—why would you?—but there's increasing evidence that areas of myocardial infarction are able to revascularize. The infarcted muscles aren't really dead. They're merely hibernating, sleeping until newly formed arteries come to awaken them with oxygen. Perhaps, the specialists agreed, the damaged area in Garek's visual cortex was trying to revascularize, too. There was even MRI evidence to support their theory, a slight but real improvement compared to studies done three years ago. So the research protocol began."

"Research?"

"Revascularizing infarcted brain is even more cutting-edge than revascularizing hearts. But there's this promising experimental drug. The one they infuse that causes such pain. Garek gets the potent potion via arteriogram every thirty days, followed three days later by an MRI—a piece of cake by contrast, coffinlike contraption though it is."

"And?"

"And nothing. Well, *pain*, which he doesn't admit to, and hope, which he *did* mention, he couldn't help it, at first. *Everyone* was ecstatic following the first arteriogram. No caution at all in the optimistic raves. The lights he'd been seeing became even brighter, uncomfortably so, like staring directly into the sun. And there were shadows, *shapes*, in the sunny brilliance. The glaring brightness faded within twenty-four hours, but the enthusiasm didn't. The doctors expected the brilliance to fade. But it would return, they predicted, with each successive dose, and it would linger longer each time, and the shapes and shadows would become ever more clear, and by the end of six months he would be well on his way to the eventual recovery of his sight."

"But that didn't happen? The cumulative effect?" *Oh, Garek, why not?*

"No. The uncomfortable brightness came on cue. Still does, I gather. But it faded as swiftly on successive treatments as it did on the first. By the third go-round it was obvious the potion wasn't going to work. Not for Garek. But he'd committed to the full protocol, the six arteriograms followed by six MRIs. So there he is. At the hospital. Today of all days."

"But coming back this evening? Shouldn't he be spending the night?"

"Of course he should be! Especially since the *worst* part of the entire fiasco begins at nine tonight, when he gets the antidote, the *rescue*. There it is, that word again. But that's what it's called, and what it *does*. The research compound is both potent *and* toxic. Medicine and poison. It needs to be neutralized exactly eight hours after each infusion is complete. The rescue concept isn't new. It's been used in cancer therapy for decades. In that instance, the rapidly growing tumor cells take up the medicine more quickly and in larger amounts than the normal cells do. As a result of such greediness, they receive the most poison and die. If not rescued in time, however, some of the normal cells would meet a similar fate. No one's killing cells in Garek's brain, *au contraire*, but the principle's the same. The cells that are industriously making new blood vessels take up the research compound first, and use it productively. But because the medicine is poison, too, the rescue drug must be given."

"And is worse, even, than the arteriogram?"

"Much worse, according to my not-prone-to-embellish hospital source. Every cell in the body reacts with sheer relief at being rescued. Joy for the cells. More discomfort for Garek. Severe nausea, apparently, and aching, cramping, *everywhere*, paroxysms of both that come and go throughout the night."

"Who's with him during the rescue, Olympia?" *Who takes care of the rescuer?*

"Who do you think? *No one.* Garek gives himself the infusion at nine. It's intravenous, through a line they put in his arm before sending him home. The rescue medicine is in a preloaded syringe, and Garek knows immediately whether it's been injected where it's supposed to be—his bloodstream—because the relieved cells react at once."

"And if something goes wrong?"

"He insists that it won't. Can't. And, after consultation with my source, I have to admit I'm inclined to agree."

"But someone should be with him, checking on him, helping him." *Loving him.*

"He doesn't want that. And, medically, it's not necessary. He was hospitalized the first time, of course. His vital signs were absolutely stable. And, since he's declined to take any drugs to counteract the rescue symptoms—with his doctors' blessings, by the way, the fewer meds in his bloodstream during the rescue the better—there's really nothing for the hospital personnel to do. Except watch him. Which, even if sighted, I'm quite sure he would hate, and unsighted, being watched without knowing he's being watched, especially when he's having paroxysms of pain . . . well, I can understand why *that* has no appeal."

"So can I. You said you'd be talking to him again before you leave?"

"Definitely."

"Will you tell him I know about the arteriogram, and that if he wants to cancel this evening, that's fine? We can meet tomorrow, or whenever's best for him."

"I'll tell him, Giselle. But he won't cancel. Won't *want* to. Not Garek. Not tonight."

FOURTEEN

*G*arek didn't call. Didn't cancel. As Olympia had promised he would not.

Olympia called, however, shortly after five. Yes, she was leaving. Yes, she *did* see that snowflake.

Garek, too, was leaving. The hospital. A little later than usual, Olympia confided, because of some extra bleeding at the arterial puncture site in his leg. Yes, he'd be able to sit by seven-thirty and walk *short* distances, too. But he'd be lying down, Olympia said, he'd better be, between his return to the Towers and Giselle's arrival at his penthouse door.

Olympia revealed without revealing details that they knew where Grace was living, and that Carolyn Logan had *wept* when she'd seen Giselle's photos of the little girl.

Olympia had left a Zip disk in Garek's penthouse, in the

office there. Its only file—"GAQ"—contained the complete Grace Alysia Quinn investigation, from interviews last fall in Loganville to every morsel of information gathered today.

Olympia hadn't been certain she'd be able to get everything typed and organized before the snow. But since she had, would Giselle please let Garek know?

Yes, Giselle assured her. Of course she would.

Then Olympia was gone. In plenty of time, Giselle thought, to get home safely. The snow began in earnest, and so beautifully, at six-thirty. Rambunctious angels were frolicking with feather pillows once again.

Pastel feathers, myriad pillows.

By seven-fifteen, when she began her journey to Garek's penthouse, shimmering rainbows blanketed the world.

Giselle used the codes Olympia had given her, needed to, and reached the Towers' lobby with six minutes to spare. As her snow chimes fluttered overhead, she studied the building directory posted on a marble wall.

Only the commercial residents were listed, the businesses that occupied the first twenty-two floors. Garek's law office was there, as was WCHM radio and TV.

Did Kathleen work at WCHM still? And did the popular radio personality still live on one of the building's uppermost floors?

Did Kathleen *see* Garek sometimes, without his knowing he was being seen? Masked, as he was, by his blindness?

Giselle ascended to the Towers' top floor at 7:29. The penthouse door opened before she rang the bell.

And there he was. The man she loved. More handsome

even than he'd been in the mists and magic of Venice. So handsome. But thin. And pale.

His hair was long for an attorney, and longer still for the ex-SEAL who hadn't quite been able to kick rescuer habit— until the mask of darkness had given him no choice.

But the lustrous hair wasn't so terribly long, Giselle thought, Giselle ached, for a man who could not see. Just as, for such a man, Garek was neither surprisingly thin nor shockingly pale.

Like eating, or running for miles along Lake Shore Drive, maintaining a fashionable haircut had become, with his blindness, far more than just a mild but necessary bother.

He wasn't diligent about haircuts, this man who could not see, any more than he made sure his once powerful body was adequately fed, or—

Wait a minute. This man who could not see?

His eyes found hers. Those blue, blue eyes. Gentle and dark, caressing and dangerous.

A depthless ocean of deceit.

If Kathleen's not pregnant, you will hear from me.

And now, before her . . .

"Yes, I am," he said quietly. "Quite blind."

But reading my thoughts, my Garek, my love. Seeing my thoughts still.

"Hello, Giselle."

"Hello, Garek."

"Please come in."

"Thank you."

She stepped onto the plush carpet that had been vacuumed just for her, and, for her, into a glow as luminous and golden as the Venetian moon.

"Olympia says you don't need a tour."

"No. She also says you shouldn't be walking. Much."

"I won't be. Much. I'm fine."

She wanted to touch him, this man she'd never touched, and never let him go—as Garek had promised, harsh and low, that if he held her, if he dared, it would be forever.

Giselle didn't touch. Did not dare. And so lightly, so brightly, she said, "Well, I'm *not* fine. There's way too much light. I feel as if I'm looking straight into the sun. Do you?"

"I do, but only for a few more hours. You and Olympia had quite a chat."

"She's lovely."

"Yes, she is."

"So may I get rid of some of this glare?" *This golden brilliance you've created for me despite the discomfort—and the torment—it causes you?*

"Sure. Or I can."

"No, Garek McIntyre. You're sitting, remember?"

"I remember. I'm sitting."

He sat on one of twin sofas in the living room. But he didn't relax, not while she was standing.

Giselle moved quickly, dousing the many lights, and being watched, followed, by his sightless blue eyes. He sensed, somehow, her near-silent mission. Sensed *her*? Or was it only that his aching eyes sought respite from the painful glare by seeking the solace of dark shadows?

Dark shadows, Giselle realized when the golden lights glowed no more. Shadows. Darkness. But not *blackness*. The falling crystals of snow captured the nighttime brilliance of the city below, a brightness that was enhanced, by design, by the mirrored walls within.

Only when Giselle pulled closed the heavy drapes was every lumen of snow light, of snow magic, extinguished.

"There," she said. "Is that better?"

"For me. Yes. But a little dark, I should think, for you."

"I'm fine, Garek!" *Fine*, with her perfect eyes. A visitor, only, to this darkness. It was *so* dark, this darkness. His darkness. Even with her perfect eyes, she had yet to discern shades of ebony in this moonless night. "This must be so difficult for you."

"I hate it, Giselle."

His voice held no bitterness. No self-pity. No rage. Just the quiet, simple, *and so complicated* truth.

"I hate it for you."

"I have no one to blame but myself."

"Don't you?" How about the glass sculptress who told you about a girl named Gigi just hours before that Balkan dawn? A girl who, you insisted, had been repeatedly raped? Mightn't Gigi have been in your thoughts when it came to rescuing another ravaged, truly ravaged, innocent?

Giselle didn't embellish her *Don't you?* aloud. Garek knew what she was asking.

His reply was swift and sure. "No, Giselle. I don't." Then softly, "Thanks only to myself, I'm a wee bit more blind than I'd like to be. But I'm fine. And very grateful to you that we've found Grace."

He was thanking her for the luminous brightness of finding Grace, not the darkness she had caused. And in the softness of his words Giselle heard even more.

They were here, on this snowy night, because of Grace. *Grace*, not Garek, not Giselle. Not Garek *and* Giselle.

But Garek and Giselle existed still. And they would talk, they *would*, another time.

These ninety minutes, however, this time before Garek—alone—would rescue his dying cells, Garek and Giselle together would try to rescue Grace.

Giselle found with her hands the sofa that was the twin to his, and sat across from him, not seeing him yet, but feeling so safe in the blackness because he was there.

"Olympia says you know where Grace is."

"I do. And I'll tell you. But will you tell me first about the six days she was with you in New Orleans?"

"Of course, although I doubt she'd remember any of it."

"Tell me anyway. Her tugging you to the photo booth suggests that at least some of her memories weren't entirely lost."

"Okay. Well. I first saw her at five o'clock on the afternoon of the eighteenth. She was standing on the sidewalk outside the clinics entrance of the county hospital. My mother was standing a few feet away. I told you in Venice about my mother's addiction to heroin."

"She was desperately addicted, you said. An addiction of despair."

Giselle saw light, now, in the blackness. Light from two sources. The first, and paler of the two, came *from Dawn*. The sculpture glowed gold, as if illuminated by a remnant of fire trapped within the once-molten glass.

The second light, the brighter fire, was brilliant blue, and came from him.

"You remember," she whispered.

She saw flickers in the deep blue flames of his deep blue eyes, intense glitters of pure surprise. Had she really imagined he'd forget even a single word?

"You and your mother must have been just about to leave for Venice." *For Carnivale. For Armande.*

The fire darkened, then disappeared.

But Garek was waiting in the blackness, listening for more words he would not forget.

"In ten days," Giselle replied. "On the twenty-eighth. That's why she was at the clinic. She'd be getting follow-up care in Venice, it was already arranged, but it made sense to begin her opiate withdrawal in New Orleans. The methadone clinic personnel knew her well, and despite her past failures were willing to take her back. She was so optimistic about success this time, about the healing powers of Venice. That January eighteenth was her fourth day of methadone. She was receiving a large dose, she needed to be, and was very groggy as a result. That's why she was standing on the sidewalk, waiting for me to escort her home. I noticed Grace, of course, as I approached. A spaced-out girl all alone. She was a cancer patient, I decided, waiting for her ride in lieu of making the short but exhausting walk to the parking garage."

"You didn't see Troy."

"No. But he certainly could have been nearby. I wouldn't have noticed. I was focused on my mother, and on Grace. I have no way of knowing whether the man who spoke to my mother even *was* Troy. She described him to me only as he'd described himself to her, as a shrimper from the Gulf. Troy might have hired such a man, the real thing, told him what to say and paid him well to say it. Although . . ."

"Not Troy Logan's style? I agree. He'd have wanted to tell the stories, spin the lies, himself. He wouldn't have missed it for the world."

"He was a monster."

"Yes, he was."

"Who probably *was* watching. If so, he would have seen my mother rouse herself from her stupor as I started to guide her away. The girl was coming with us, she said. *Insisted.* In fact, in a moment of sheer clarity, as it turns out, she took custody of the cosmetics case Grace carried. I took custody of Grace. Over the next few hours, in a vague and rambling narrative, my mother told me what the shrimper—Troy—had told her. The girl had lost both her parents in the weeks before Christmas. Her father died first, stabbed to death in a barroom brawl, and her grief-stricken mother jumped to her death on Christmas Eve."

"With her daughter in tow?"

"Yes. Which is how Troy explained her muteness, her amnesia, her shaved head. The neurosurgeons were *going* to operate, he said. But they decided at the last minute there wasn't a need to after all. Just as there was no need for Troy to shave off all her hair. True, what was growing back was brown not gold. But no one was searching, then, for Grace Alysia Quinn. It was cruelty, I think. Monstrousness. Her hair color really did change, though, didn't it? Dramatically."

"Which can happen, according to Olympia, who made some calls. Grace's color would likely have darkened with age. The trauma she sustained, both physical and emotional, merely accelerated the process. Just as trauma in adults can turn hair prematurely gray."

Did he know, Giselle wondered, that his own long lustrous hair was dark brown still? Had the ex-SEAL challenged the color not to succumb to the trauma? Had he *forbidden* it to?

This is about Grace, she reminded herself. Tonight is about saving Grace.

Who needed desperately to be saved.

"After telling his fiction about Grace's past, Troy proceeded to doom her future. I repeated his lie to the orphanage personnel, who in time shared it with her."

"You had to repeat it, Giselle. Just as they did."

"We all did precisely what he wanted us to do, didn't we? Of course, he stacked the deck strongly in his favor, giving Grace to an obvious addict *and* sprinkling in a rather spectacular incentive as well."

"Money."

"Twenty-nine thousand five hundred ninety-five dollars and twenty cents. In the cosmetics case. The bills were old, circulated, bound by rubber bands. And the coins, two nickels and a dime, were in a plastic sandwich bag. Does that amount, those numbers, have any significance?"

"None that I know of. Not offhand. I'll have them checked, though. It's just a matter of entering relevant birth dates, anniversaries, and so on into a search-and-scramble program. My guess would be we won't find anything, that it's simply the amount, less expenses, that Troy had with him when he left Loganville with Grace. According to Carolyn, he routinely kept tens of thousands in cash at his home."

"Pocket change, even twenty-three years ago, to a man as wealthy as Troy. But a fortune to my mother. She didn't know how much money would be in the cosmetics case until she opened it at Monique's, only that Troy had promised it was a lot."

"Which he explained how?"

"They were his neighbors, he said. The girl and her parents. They lived in a neighboring shack and in comparable poverty. But when he'd gone into his dead neighbors' home in search of a familiar nightgown for the hospitalized girl, he'd discovered they hadn't been as impoverished as he'd believed. The plastic bag in which he found the coins, coupled with a supply of such bags and the large amount of cash, suggested that the father had been dealing drugs. Troy—as the poor shrimper—said he'd considered keeping the money himself. No one would ever know. Instead, as if stricken with conscience, he pretended to be the girl's only living relative. He'd care for her, he told her doctors, when she was ready to go home. Implausible, really, isn't it? That a hospital would have released her so casually?"

"I'm not sure it's implausible at all. Besides, from your standpoint, and from your mother's, there he was, at another hospital, in the hope of finding specialized care for her, I imagine, in New Orleans?"

"That's what he said. He was almost inside when he spotted my mother—who looked, he claimed, *exactly* like the beloved mother the girl had lost. A lie, of course. But Amy Louise Trent looked exactly like who she was, an addict and a prostitute."

"A victim, Giselle."

"A victim," she echoed in the blackness. "Who wouldn't have gone to the police in a million years, no matter what crime had been committed. Not, in a million years, that it would have occurred to any of us there'd even been a crime."

"Why would it? The money spoke volumes, over twenty-nine thousand reasons to believe every word Troy said. Over twenty-nine thousand reasons," Garek said softly, "for your mother to run away."

"She left that night with Grace's money and Monique's brooch. Even if the banks had been open, we—I—would never have thought of taking the money there. Neither my mother nor I even had a bank account. Monique did, of course, as well as a safe within the mansion. But both were inaccessible without Monique, who was in Savannah until morning."

"Besides," he said, "you believed your mother wanted to go to Venice."

"I really did. And the idea that my mother would steal an inheritance from an orphaned little girl . . . well, as we've previously established, I was hopelessly trusting in those days."

"She was your mother, Giselle. You loved her, believed in her."

"And I even believed that she loved me. She could have taken us with her, Garek. The three of us could have made a new start. Instead she took all but twenty cents of the twenty-nine thousand five hundred ninety-five chances we had."

"She left the coins?"

"By accident, Monique raged when she returned from Georgia."

"But you think it was intentional, don't you? Sentimental. Like her taking Monique's brooch and your sketch of Venice."

"I do think that. *Still.* The coins were the only tangible symbol the girl would have of the life, the mother, she'd lost. My mother was not so sentimental, however, when it came to the Valium."

"Which wasn't, I would guess, in a prescription bottle."

"No. A blank envelope. Troy had told my mother the dose the girl was to receive. One tablet four times a day until the pills were gone. They were ten-milligram tablets. I'd seen enough Valium to know. A huge dose for a little girl."

"And even for Carolyn Logan, who'd never taken Valium before, but who at Troy's insistence was on forty milligrams a day following the Christmas Eve inferno."

"He was snowing them both."

"And, in Grace's case, preventing her from making new memories until he was long gone. High-dose Valium can induce amnesia even when the recipient is awake."

"Like during an arteriogram?"

"So they say." Garek didn't say, didn't need to, that he'd declined such memory annihilation for himself. "Did you get more Valium for Grace?"

"No. Monique could have gotten more, but she was focused on the bigger picture, obsessed with punishing my mother at first, then once diverted on salvaging what she could. She set up a trust fund for Grace and arranged for her to be placed in what she claimed was the best private orphanage that she—or anyone—could find. I wanted to take Grace with me to Venice. If *my* mother looked like *hers*, I reasoned, then I looked like that beloved lost mother, too.

But Monique held all the cards, and Monique said no. Which, given that it was all a lie, was undoubtedly for the best. An orphanage in the States, not a palazzo in Venice with me."

A palazzo in Venice *with Armande*, Garek amended in silence. In darkness. I know, my Giselle, how magical Venice is with you. How healing, how lovely, how bright.

"How bad has her life been?" Giselle asked.

"Not bad at all from what we can tell. The orphanage really was the best, and she enjoyed school, loved it and excelled, up to and including a master's degree. The trust fund was expertly managed, and by the time it became hers, at the end of your ten-year agreement with Monique, it was all the money she would ever need. She's touched the interest only, and only rarely. But her fortune is there, Giselle. The fortune you gave her. It's given her the freedom to live as she likes, and to make changes when she chooses."

"We're about to make a monumental change for her. Someone is."

"Yes. And I'd like to discuss with you just who that someone might be . . ."

FIFTEEN

ain. Rain.

Rain.

Pierce watched the torrent from his home atop the Towers.

The play of city lights with dancing raindrops created a waterfall of gemstones, of emeralds mostly, because of the lights that shone beneath his view.

Emerald raindrops. Like the glassy green that spilled, chiming, in Seattle's Wind Chimes Hotel. Giselle had been right to spin emerald rain for the Emerald City. Just as it had been inspired for the San Francisco hotel, whimsical yet dazzling, to create a fleet of little cable cars, climbing and chiming halfway to a galaxy of stars. And Giselle's decision for the Dallas Wind Chimes—

Nice try, Pierce told himself. This effort to guide his thoughts away from Anastasia. But the effort was quite futile. His brain—or was it his heart?—was not so easily outfoxed.

Especially when his mental segue had taken him from emerald rain to wind chimes of glass to the artistry of Giselle—who'd be creating his skater. His Anastasia.

Giselle was not the way to *not* think about Anastasia. So what was? Nothing. All thoughts led to the lost princess. One degree of separation, no matter how disconnected the thoughts might seem.

So he surrendered as he gazed at the weeping emerald sky. He thought, simply, about her.

She hadn't called. Hadn't returned his call. And she'd definitely gotten his message. Mrs. Holt had given it to her this morning as promised.

She was feeling *much* better, Mrs. Holt reported when Pierce called the school to check. No, she wasn't coming in. No sense in risking a relapse, especially since she seemed on the road to recovery.

Besides, Mrs. Holt noted, the first nationally televised special about Grace was being broadcast from nine to ten tonight, an entire hour of prime time devoted to the lost little girl.

Not only did the recuperating-but-still-under-the-weather librarian need to be in Mrs. Holt's words "bright-eyed and bushy-tailed" for that, but she was expecting an important and related delivery to her condominium some-time before noon.

Yes, the Canterbury's building manager *could* accept the

delivery, and with Anastasia's advance permission could even open her condo door. But it would be best if she personally oversaw the installation of her new television and VCR, learning as she did how everything worked.

It was really above and beyond the call of duty, Mrs. Holt asserted, for the dedicated librarian—and book-club hostess—to make such purchases.

Mrs. Holt herself wouldn't be staying up for the special. She was the early-to-bed early-to-rise type. But she'd be recording it, her husband would be, so in the event Anastasia's new VCR didn't work a backup would be available.

"There will actually be," Mrs. Holt added, "whatever eighteen times six is, given that every girl in every class will be recording the special, too. Although, since we have several *sisters* in the school, it would be eighteen times six minus whatever, *plus* the faculty and staff will be recording . . . well, suffice to say, *many* copies will be made."

Mrs. Holt didn't do the math in her head. Nor did Pierce. Nor did he call the sister, his own, who could have done so in a flash. Including, in a flash, making appropriate subtractions for families with multiple Peggys.

He'd spoken with Val recently. Last night. She'd updated him on the newlyweds, honeymooning in Maui, marveling at the whales, the tropics, their wedding vows, and calling home with amazing and gratifying frequency to share their joy.

Pierce had given Val an update as well. Yes, as was being reported, the construction crew had returned to Carillon Square. And it did mean, as had been speculated, that the Carillon problem, invisible to all but Pierce, had been solved.

Pierce shared the solution, but not its genesis, with his sister—who raved. She could not *wait* to do a little twirling on ice herself. Skating *and* shopping, she enthused. A winning combination.

Eventually, as Pierce had known it would, the conversation had drifted to the tizzy among selected Peggy parents surrounding Grace. Val was wedded to a schoolwide book club. No field trips. No television cameras. Just the girls, their much admired librarian, and whatever family members chose to attend.

Including uncles, Val noted. *Especially* when the uncle was already involved.

Involved had been applied to him—before Anastasia—in a negative, if fondly exasperated, way. The women he'd known before Anastasia had recounted candidly, and accurately, to *Mile High* magazine the propensity for involvement, or lack thereof, of the magazine's most eligible bachelor of the year. Pierce Rourke was emotionally uncommitted, they reported. Personally uninvolved.

And on the island of dreams on Valentine's night?

Or did you mean, he had asked her, *that it isn't right— fair? wise?—for us to get involved? If so, it's too late. I am involved, Anastasia. I want to be.*

But it's not, she'd replied, *what I want!*

Involved, Val? Pierce had echoed. Finally.

Well, she'd wondered, hadn't he sent an e-mail to Garek McIntyre with an offer of help?

Yes, he had. And he'd received from Garek a gracious

reply, a thank you for his offer and the assertion that Garek might very well take him up on it should the occasion arise.

Pierce hadn't shared with Val how quickly Garek's reply had come.

But now, as he watched the rain and waited for Anastasia to return his call, Pierce reflected on the attorney's rapid response. Analyzed it.

He'd heard from Garek by return e-mail. Within a minute or two. Not enough time for even the most casual of vetting to be done. Not even the confirmation that Pierce had been the prosecutor he'd claimed to be.

Pierce had given Garek McIntyre only his legal credentials. But, he wondered, was it his architectural reputation that had prompted Garek's swift and unreserved reply?

The Windy City attorney had, after all, made a personal commitment to the structural integrity of Pierce's work, with both his home and his office in the Wind Chimes there.

Nice try, Pierce thought again. These unrelated-to-Anastasia thoughts about a man Pierce didn't even know. But Garek had segued to Wind Chimes, which flowed like emerald raindrops to Giselle, which glided on skates to Anastasia.

One degree of separation? No, Pierce thought. No separation at all. No matter where his thoughts began, they inevitability searched for Anastasia *and found her.*

When the phone rang, hope soared. And Pierce heard,

as he answered, the softness in his voice. In Liam's voice. For her. "Hello?"

"Pierce? It's Giselle."

"Giselle." Not Anastasia. But calling *about* Anastasia. Calling to tell him that . . . "You're having doubts about the skater."

"No. I'm not. I see her very clearly, Pierce. Exactly as you described her to me. Actually, I'm calling on a completely unrelated issue. I mean *completely*. So much so that if there's a logical segue, I can't imagine what it would be."

"Who needs segues? Go ahead, Giselle. I'll adjust."

"Okay. Well, I'm in Chicago with Garek McIntyre."

No adjustment was necessary. No separation at all. "The attorney who's spearheading the search for Grace."

"Yes."

And who was also on the line. After brief introductions, Garek, whose search it was, deferred to Giselle.

"We believe we've found her," she said.

"We have found her," Garek clarified. "Thanks to Giselle."

"You know her, Giselle?"

"I did know her, Pierce. Briefly. That January when Troy gave her away. He gave her to us, my mother and me, in New Orleans. She was only there for six days, but I knew where she was for the next ten years, and since she's kept the name Troy gave her, it took Garek's investigators less than a day to find out where she is now . . . and where she is, Pierce, is in Denver."

Denver, where he had searched for her would-be killer all those years ago, prayed for her, prayed for Grace.

Found grace.

And now, in Denver, Grace was found.

"This is wonderful," Pierce murmured. "Remarkable. It seemed such a long shot to find her ever, much less so quickly. Does this phone call mean I get to help?" *To help the girl who, during those icy roamings, changed my life?*

"If you'd like to."

"I'd love to. In any way I can."

"Great," Giselle said. "Thanks. We thought you would. So much so that we've already e-mailed you a file containing everything Garek and his investigators have learned from her childhood in Loganville to what's been uncovered today. We hoped, once you've had a chance to look through it, we could discuss how best, *who* best, to approach her. She won't know she's Grace. Won't have the slightest idea. And, as you'll see from the file, she'll have spent most of her life believing a malicious lie."

"I'll read the file tonight and call you when?"

"In the morning?"

"Sure. I take it you're thinking the *who best* might be someone from Denver present not Loganville past?"

"That's where our thinking is at the moment. Although, having said that, we've been wondering if it should be me. True, I'm from her past, but from *after* the fire. She might even remember me, albeit vaguely, and as Gigi not Giselle. I have photographs taken of the two of us together, as she may still have, too."

"That all sounds good."

197

"Until you factor in my role in perpetuating Troy's lie, and the emotions I'm feeling because of that. I want Grace to know the truth, *and to embrace it happily*, joyfully, tonight. This *minute*. Such urgency is very likely *not* what's best for her. As good as the truth is, it's going to be life-changing, and maybe a little life-shattering, for her."

"It might be worth discussing with a psychiatrist. I can speak with Thomas, if that's all right with you, to see what and who he recommends."

"That would be terrific, Pierce. There's undoubtedly a right way to do this. A best way. And there are reasons, as it turns out, to involve Thomas. And maybe even Val."

"Val?"

"Val *knows* her. Knows *of* her at the very least. And Val's so easy to talk to. So comfortable."

Val knows her.

There are reasons to involve Thomas.

She's lived a malicious lie.

She's kept the name Troy gave her.

The words were music to Pierce, *became* music in the silence.

"Anastasia," he whispered. "You're talking about Anastasia."

"*You* know her, Pierce? You know Anastasia Finch?"

Know her, miss her, want her, love her. "Yes."

"And do you think she's Grace?"

"I know she is, Giselle. And you know what? You get your wish. She's going to learn the truth tonight. Soon. Just as soon as I can get to her. This may or may not be the right way. The best way. But it's the way it's going to be."

For the second time in as many days Giselle heard from Pierce a solemn and unyielding certainty.

"She's your ice-skater, isn't she?" Giselle asked. "Anastasia—Grace—is your solitary ballerina reaching for the moon."

"Yes, Giselle, she is. Did she skate as a girl?"

"All winter, every winter," Garek answered, for only Garek knew the answer.

"Where?"

"There's a lake in Loganville."

"And did she sing, Garek?"

"Yes. In her home, only. And, until the weeks before the fire, only for her mother. But during those weeks of Christmas, of carols, she sang to both Mary Beth and Jace. It was Jace who told me about her singing. Which, he said, was extraordinary."

She's kept the name Troy gave her, Giselle had said. The name, Pierce thought, the psychopath had chosen with deliberate care. An old-fashioned name, at once enchanting and a little strange, and laced with clues.

Anastasia Finch. The lost princess, perhaps dead, perhaps alive, and a songbird.

"Troy must have known she sang," Pierce said. "He *must* have."

"Yes," Garek confirmed. "He did know. Whether he ever heard her sing, or only knew of her gift from her proud mother, I don't know. I do know that he wanted Grace to sing at his wedding to Carolyn, which was to have taken place two days after that Christmas Eve. Grace had already agreed to be their flower girl, but when asked to sing, she steadfastly declined to do so. All that's in the file we've sent you, and a great deal more. Every detail, no matter how trivial, faithfully transcribed."

"We'll download the file at her place, which is where I'm going now."

"Pierce." Garek's tone was command. "Let me mention one additional item before you go."

"Hold on," Pierce commanded in reply. He'd already grabbed his wallet and his keys. He made the switch from portable phone to cell phone as he strode toward the door. "All right, Garek. Go ahead."

"She had three coins when Troy left her with Giselle. We'd like to check them for prints if she has them still. There's a cosmetics case as well. Don't get me wrong. We believe she's Grace. No one's going to require proof. But belief becomes certainty—for everyone—when we find Troy's prints, or Carolyn's, on those coins or in that case."

"I'll ask, at some point, about the coins and the case. I'm not sure when that point will be, or when I'll get back to you."

"Take your time, Pierce. Let her take her time. It's been twenty-three years. We're not going to tell anyone until Grace wants us to."

"*He*'s in love with her."

"Yes." Garek's voice was very soft. "He is."

They were in Garek's penthouse office, which was shadowed, not lightless. Its view, pure lake, cast so little light that Giselle hadn't pulled the drapes.

Now, in that little light, Giselle looked at Garek's shadow, lean and tall, and awaited more words, more softness, more musings about love.

Giselle waited, lingered, as if since their mission to rescue Grace was now in the tender care of the man who loved her, she and Garek had all the time in the world. Time to wait, time to linger, time to imagine shades of meaning, shadows of promise.

Giselle did have all the time in the world. But Garek did not. Even though his silhouette, motionless and calm, suggested nothing but leisure . . . no indication whatsoever that every cell within was dying, would die, if not rescued in time.

Soon.

"Garek! It must be close to nine, if not *after*."

"Close to," Garek affirmed calmly. "My watch vibrated the eight-fifty-five signal a few minutes ago."

"A few minutes? I'd better go."

Garek didn't move. "We'll talk tomorrow, Giselle. All right? Tomorrow we'll talk."

"Yes." *Please.* "I could stay, Garek. If you like. For a while."

"No. Thank you. I'll walk you to the door."

"No. Thank *you*. I can very easily let myself out, and you must have things to . . . prepare."

The dark shadow hesitated. She did not.

"I'm letting myself out."

She heard his smile as he spoke. "Okay."

"Will you call me if you need . . ." *me?*

"I will, Giselle. But I won't." *And I do. How I do.* "I'll call you in the morning, or sooner if I hear from Pierce."

"Will that be difficult, Garek? If Pierce calls during the night?"

"Not difficult at all."

SIXTEEN

*I*t was the sort of trick one could play on a blind man, if one were so inclined—opening and closing a penthouse door without crossing the threshold at all.

Giselle hadn't planned the trick when she'd said she'd let herself out. She'd been thinking only of his recently punctured femoral artery, and of the time.

But when she opened the door, and in another step would have gone from his world of darkness to her world of light, she balked.

His world was where she wanted to be.

And where Garek didn't want her, not tonight. Not for the past three years of nights. And tomorrow night? Maybe. *Please.*

Garek would never know she'd disobeyed his wishes, the trick she'd played. She wouldn't stay the night, only a few precious minutes, crucial minutes, just long enough to be certain the rescue drug was in his bloodstream.

Garek would know right away, Olympia had said. His rescued cells would inform him. The tiny hostages would cry their relief, scream their joy.

And if some mishap occurred during the rescue? Some carelessness that resulted from caring too much? His thoughts distracted by Grace, perhaps, *or by her*?

With utter calm, despite the crisis, Garek would phone the hospital to report what had occurred. He wouldn't realize, couldn't see, that already the storm had rendered the roadways impassable—to ambulances, that is, and taxis and cars.

But not impassable to her. She'd race into the storm, dash through the billowed rainbows of snow, and retrieve for the rescuer a second rescue syringe.

Giselle closed the penthouse door as she hoped a departing guest would, an unself-conscious exit that was neither too soft nor too loud. Then, in a few soundless footfalls, she was standing in Garek's living room, seeing darkness, seeing *Dawn*, and listening, listening, for destiny.

And she heard?

Silence. Silence. Mission accomplished.

Rescue mission accomplished. The drug was in his bloodstream. No phone calls were being made. Garek McIntyre had depressed the plunger of the loaded syringe as decisively as a ravaged girl had pulled the trigger of his loaded gun.

Giselle could leave. Safely.

Should leave. Certainly.

But didn't leave. Could not.

Mightn't there be a delayed reaction? One that Olympia hadn't known about? Because her hospital source, as well informed as she might be, was unaware, they all were, of the dangers of the sixth and final rescue?

The sound was distant. From his bedroom. And faint and low.

It was the soft moan, Giselle realized, of a wounded animal believing himself to be quite alone. Such vulnerability was permissible then, when neither vultures circled overhead nor predators prowled the terrain nearby.

Permissible, and necessary, she thought. It was instinct, this controlled scream, the exhaling of what pain could be released in order to make room for more.

Instinct, not training—at least not training for a captured SEAL. He would growl, that SEAL, would be trained to do so, a warning not a confession, a declaration to his captors, his torturers, that he would fight.

But in the sanctuary of his penthouse lair, amid a sky of falling rainbows, the blinded beast could moan softly, safely.

Privately.

Giselle hated the sound, his solitude, her intrusion, his pain. But it brought comfort, too, proof that the rescue drug was where it belonged and doing its rescuing.

The moaning stopped abruptly. And utterly.

Paroxysms, Olympia had said. Frenzies of discomfort interspersed with respites of reprieve. Giselle wanted the respites for Garek. Far more respites than frenzies. Quiet times in which to rest, to recover, to prepare for the next onslaught.

Quiet times.

But, Giselle thought, this sudden silence felt *more* than quiet. Ominously still. Excessively hushed.

And dark. And deep.

What if, in their exuberant relief, the cells of his heart had begun to dance in a rhythm too wild to endure? An arrhythmia, not a rhythm at all, that was silently, frantically, incompatible with life?

"I don't blame you, Giselle."

"*Garek.*" He was so close to her, this stealthy night warrior. Had he been an ancient assassin, wielding a Venetian dagger, his victim's death, *her* death, would have been instantly assured. "I'm *sorry*. I just wanted to make sure the infusion went without incident, to *be* here in case there was a problem, because of the storm. I *know* I should have left by now, shouldn't have stayed in the first place. I know how private this is . . . you are."

"I meant," Garek McIntyre said softly, "I don't blame you for my blindness."

"Oh." *Oh.* "But you *should* blame me, shouldn't you? She was dying, *going* to die. You should have left her there. You knew that, didn't you? You *knew* there was no hope?"

"I knew." He drew a ragged breath of pure instinct, the injured animal being ravaged anew by this rescue that came with such pain. When he exhaled at last, Giselle heard a raw edge, and a gentle smile. "And now that I think of it, what I said wasn't entirely accurate. I don't *blame* you for

206

my blindness. But it *is* your fault. You're the reason I didn't leave her, couldn't leave her to die all alone in that hell. I was a better man, Giselle, a much better man that morning because of you."

"Oh, Garek." Relief and rescue ripped through her, too. Relief. Rescue. Pain. "You promised me, *promised me,* that if Kathleen wasn't pregnant—"

"*I was blind.*"

His sightless eyes glittered brilliant blue, fire intense. It was a warrior's gaze, fierce and daunting, but it was matched, spark for spark, by the impassioned brightness of hers.

"Did you really believe your blindness would have made a difference to me? Other than hating it *for you*?"

"No." The blazing blue became a tender caress. "I believed it *wouldn't* have made a difference. Even though it should have. Our love was just beginning."

"Just beginning, Garek? We'd had six hours *and twenty years*. You said so yourself."

"I know, and I believed it then. I believed everything then, Giselle. But all we really had was mists and magic, desire and destiny, and six hours—only six that I could truly count when I counted, *re*-counted, in my darkness. I wasn't the man you'd met, you'd known."

"A *better* man you said."

"And a worse one. It was eight months before I was able to get out of the hospital and *stay* out. Eight months. And a very long time after that before I knew how dependent I'd need to be, and how independent I could be."

Garek is his own eyes, Olympia had said. The loner had

207

pushed himself, challenged himself, relied on himself. And? He'd survived brilliantly as always. And, as always, he'd survived alone.

"Did you ever think about us?"

"Us. You. All the time. I knew you'd assume that Kathleen had been pregnant, as I'd imagined she might be."

"What if I'd *called* you, Garek? Just to say hi?"

"I knew you wouldn't."

"But if I had?"

"I would have confirmed what you'd assumed."

"You didn't confirm last night. Didn't *lie*. You could have. I never would have known. But you didn't."

Garek didn't answer at once, and the glittering blue fire was no more. He was fighting, Giselle realized, his eyes closed in concentration as he focused everything he had on battling a fresh attack from relieved but scolding cells.

He didn't moan, not even softly. His eyes remained closed, the battle raging still, when he spoke again.

"I decided, last August, to put my practice on hold for a while. I'd find a hotel room in Carmel, I thought, and I'd date you, court you. I knew by then the man I was going to be, what I could do, what I couldn't. I'd call you first, of course, to see if you were interested still. But before I called you, Jace called me. Troy was dead, and Grace was alive, and in the midst of searching for her came the possibility that in six months I might be able to see, even a little . . ."

"Garek?"

"Yes?"

"I'm interested. *Still*."

His eyes opened, glittered, smiled . . . and kept smiling even as every cell in his body screamed as one.

Eventually the smile had to fade.

"I need you to leave, Giselle."

"Leave?"

"This is something I need to do alone, to see through by myself." The paroxysm was tearing him apart. But his voice remained intact, strong—and so gentle—for her. "Let me come to you in the morning. Please. Let me come to you at dawn."

SEVENTEEN

ain. Rain. Rain.

Which froze, every emerald drop, the moment it splashed to earth. The streets turned to ice, treacherous, unforgiving, demanding caution from even the most expert—and restless—of drivers.

Pierce, expert and restless, exercised caution even on days when driving conditions were ideal, making it a practice even then never to use his phone. The benefits, in his view, simply didn't outweigh the risks: an unfortunate accident, a preventable murder, a motherless son.

That was Pierce Rourke's standard for caution in daylight, when conditions were ideal. And on this sodden night of icy peril?

Pierce placed the first cell-phone call to Anastasia before leaving the Towers parking garage, discovering only when he emerged from the covered cocoon the ice rink Denver had become.

And hanging up upon making that discovery? No. But exercising extreme caution, and icy expertise, during the many more unanswered rings. He tried a mile later, and again later, and later still.

And the benefit of these potentially perilous calls? None. He grew ever more restless.

And the risk? He grew ever more restless.

Her phone, he told himself, was still set on mute, a forgotten vestige of Mrs. Holt's insistence that she silence the ringer so that she might rest undisturbed, might dream uninterrupted.

Which, according to Mrs. Holt, she had. Anastasia was much better, Mrs. Holt had reported. Much recovered from her terrible cold.

And from her terrible coldness?

The thought prodded Pierce's restlessness with ice-sharp spurs, and his mind's eye saw ever more clearly an image he didn't want to see.

It was a horror-movie vision, an alien creature trapped within an unsuspecting human. The creature, a grotesqueness of slimy scales and fearsome fangs, gnawed and clawed its way out, ripping, shredding, destroying as it did.

Pierce didn't want to see the image at all, much less to cast Grace in the alien's role. The demon's role. He cast the lovely innocent as a shadow instead, one with substance, five years of lost memory, lost life, lost love, and with determination to be heard, to be known, to be free.

They were one. Anastasia and Grace. But until Anastasia acknowledged that truth, the lost princess and her shadow were at war.

Pierce's cell phone rang eighty minutes into what should have been a thirty-minute drive. He was almost there. The lights of the Canterbury glowed straight ahead. He had merely to navigate a frozen yet thankfully vacant intersection.

Pierce almost didn't answer. But on this night of such slippery danger, Val might need him, or Callie, or Edward, or Lilah.

He *was* needed. Liam was needed. He felt her need despite the silence, heard her shivering fear even though she was mute.

"Anastasia," he greeted, welcomed. Liam welcomed. "Hello."

Then, to the frightened shadow within her, Pierce gently queried, "You're cold, aren't you? Too cold to speak. That's okay. Really. *You're* okay. I promise. I *promise.*"

Then as Liam again, and so softly, "It's gladness, Anastasia. I know it doesn't feel like it, but it is, believe me, it is. *It will be.* Gladness, not madness. I'll tell you all about it. Soon. I'm here, Anastasia, at your condo. It's icy in the parking lot, like at the lake, like at the Island, like in your dream. You're a far better skater than I. But you know what? I'm doing pretty well, gliding right along. In fact, it's time to buzz me in. Now. Anastasia, will you buzz— good. *Good.*"

But it wasn't good. She wasn't. *Grace* wasn't . . . which meant, for Anastasia, there was sheer terror.

Her lips were blue. Quivering. Her skin was ashen. Ice. And her hair, long and flowing, shimmered blond not sable, as if the traumatic darkening had been reversed, as if she'd journeyed back to that Christmas morning and was awakening, bewildered and cold, from her night of unconsciousness in a drift of snow.

Her eyes were as gray as the smoke from which, gasping, Grace had leapt. Gray, and clouded with ghastly images only she could see. But could she see him as well? And could she recognize him *as him*?

Pierce knew only that Anastasia didn't resist his embrace. She fell into him not away, too weak perhaps, too helpless, to struggle. And yet, Pierce believed, she wasn't afraid of him. Somewhere, deep within, she knew not to be.

He drew her shivering body close to his, and closer still, and even closer, wrapping her in his warmth, his heat.

"You're going to be all right. You're going to be *just fine*. You're getting warmer already. I can feel it. *Much* warmer. Stay with me, okay? *Stay with me.* You're loved, you know. *So very loved.*"

He whispered, he cherished, he caressed, he implored. But Pierce did not speak the words he wanted most to speak: I love you, Anastasia, *I love you.*

He didn't even speak her name. Didn't dare. Not either name.

Which name would she know? Which would help? And which, like his confession of love, could further confuse— and make her more cold?

Colder would kill her. Even a fraction of a degree. She

wasn't getting warmer. That was a wistful wish, a necessary lie. What Pierce held in his arms was quaking ice, and what he felt against his chest was a heart so cold it barely beat.

A dying heart. An agonal one.

A lovely heart that was saying good-bye.

It was then that Liam Rourke began to sing.

He sang the songs of Ireland in the voice of Ireland, lilting and magical and true.

Liam the man sang to Anastasia the woman, as Gabriel had sung to his love, his Eileen. And Liam's shadow, the lost son within, sang to the trembling shadow that was Grace.

Both heard the songs that Liam sang. Both Anastasia and Grace. And, as they did, their single heart began to beat in tempo with his, warmer, stronger, faster . . . free.

And when Anastasia looked up to him, he saw no clouds in her eyes, and no terror. But confusion still? No.

None.

"Liam," she whispered. "*Liam.*"

Her lips, no longer blue, sought his. And his lips, no longer singing, but singing always to her, welcomed her kiss, cherished it.

"Make love to me, Liam. Please. Make love to me."

"I will," he promised. "Forever."

Anastasia pulled away, just a little. But the scant distance was more than enough for a reminder of madness to wedge its way in.

"But I don't *have* forever. I only have now. And I only have that because you got here in time."

Was that true? Pierce didn't know. Didn't *want* to know. He wanted to believe that Anastasia would have survived this remembered time in the Loganville snow just as she'd survived, as Grace had survived, the first.

This remembered time, and final time.

"What happened to you this evening is never going to happen again."

"You can't know that!"

"But I can, Anastasia. And I do. You'll know it, too. Soon. I'd like to ask you a few questions first, before telling you what I know."

"But . . ."

"Trust me?"

"I do, Liam. I will."

She'd already made a nest for herself, his lovely song-bird, a haven of blankets on her living-room couch. Pierce settled her there, all the while touching her, until, to retrieve a fallen layer of fleece, he touched no more.

Anastasia shivered at once. *Shook* despite the ambient warmth, the hothouse heat, the thermostat set for violets.

She was like a pioneer in outer space, a frontierswoman exploring that last frontier, and, intrepid voyager that she was, she'd ventured outside her spacecraft to make repairs. She floated as she worked in the vast wasteland of weightlessness, of blackness, of soaring speed—tethered only by a floating rope. And if the rope snapped? She'd be gone in a gasp, lost forever.

Anastasia was that precarious, and Pierce was her floating rope, her only lifeline.

Her shivering stopped when he touched her, when he

tethered her anew to his warmth. But she was so cold, still, from her fleeting journey in outer, outer space.

I will make love to you, he'd promised. Forever. But even as he'd spoken the wondrous vow, he had thought, Not now, not yet. Not until Anastasia was tethered securely to the truth, and could come to him willingly, wantingly—maybe wantonly—not wistfully, not desperately, not believing it was a final chance at gladness before madness. Or death.

And now? When she'd become so cold again, and he could fill her, warm her, heat her with his love?

As he felt her icy cheeks warm to his touch, Pierce reaffirmed his silent vow to wait. Then taking her hands in his, he created a nest of gentleness for her there.

"What memories do you have of your parents?"

"My parents? None, really. I know only what I was told. My father was killed in a tavern when I was eight. A few weeks later, in her grief and her madness, my mother jumped, with me, from a bridge. She died instantly. My only injuries were to my head. My memory. I have total amnesia for my life before our leap—or, I suppose I should say, before our flight. I've always imagined that in her madness she believed we would fly, not fall. We were finches after all. I'm remembering that head injury, aren't I? *Feeling* it."

"I think so."

Her nod was very Miss Finch, the scholarly librarian assessing the facts. But the nod itself, the ripples it caused in her long mane of hair, shimmered pure gold. And her

216

musical voice, her wishing voice, was Anastasia. "I think so, too."

"You told me, the day we met, that you'd never been to Denver before, despite your Island dream déjà vu."

"Yes, that's right. I never had been."

"Why did you move here?"

"Because after the episode with the tainted lemonade Boston no longer felt safe. It *had* felt safe. Always. Safe. Home."

"But why Denver?"

"I don't know. It just felt . . . right."

"Safe, Anastasia? Like home?" Like *almost* home? Almost Loganville?

"The Island felt like home."

It is your home, Anastasia. Your home, our home, if that's what you want.

"Liam?"

"A couple more questions, then I'll explain. Do you have photos taken of yourself as a child with a teenage girl?"

"Yes. But I don't even know who she is, who she was— *Gigi*." Her right hand flew slowly, gracefully, from the nest of his. It fluttered first to her hair, brushing away an errant strand of silk, then glided to her temple, lighting there, perched beside her frown. "I've never remembered that before. It's probably wrong."

"No, Anastasia. It's absolutely right. She was Gigi. You had, when you knew her, two nickels and a dime."

"My mother's coins. I have them still."

"And a cosmetics case, too?"

"Yes. Liam . . ."

"Do you remember your name?"

"*My* name?"

"Yes," he said. So softly. "The name that was yours, and by which you were so very loved, for the first six years of your life. You were six, not eight, when you injured your head, when you flew by yourself on Christmas Eve. I think you've wondered about that name. Haven't you?"

"Yes," she whispered. "I have wondered. Wanted. *Wished.* As I'm sure many women have this week. But . . ." The hand at her temple left its perch to gesture to the neat stacks of articles on her living-room floor, and her copy of *People*, and the lined yellow tablets and many-colored index cards on which she'd organized for book club her meticulous notes. "I've read every article, studied every photograph, again and again. Nothing's familiar to me. *Nothing.* Grace had a head injury. I had a head injury. That's all."

"There's more for you to read and study, Anastasia. A detailed file of reminiscences and revelations from Loganville. I haven't read it, but I know a little of what it contains. I know, for instance, that Grace sang as a girl. Her voice was extraordinary even then. And even then she was a modest songstress, not a diva-to-be. She sang only for her loved ones in the privacy of her home. Troy Logan wanted her to sing at his wedding, but she refused."

"Which explains why, years later, she would sing at the weddings of strangers? As if in some subconscious spite?"

"That doesn't sound like Grace, does it? Or you. I think her subconscious was choosing joy over revenge, generosity over vengeance. She'd lost her own loved ones, but

chose to share her gift with other families celebrating love."
Pierce paused, waited. But the songstress was silent. "Grace
was also an avid ice-skater. There's a lake in Loganville
where she skated. I wonder how much it looks like the
Island's lake."

"It *doesn't*. Not at all. There's a virtual photo album of
Loganville at the web site. None of the photographs, including the many taken at the lake, is familiar to me in
any way."

"But still you've wondered, wanted, wished."

"Imagined," Anastasia clarified. "*Fantasized*. It's a fantasy, I realize, that's been going on for quite some time.
Months. Since August."

"You mean July."

"No. I drank the lemonade then, and until this week I
truly believed I'd awakened the following morning with a
pounding headache and shivering cold. But that was such
a confusing time, such a blurry time, it's not surprising I
misremembered the chronology of my symptoms. They
must have actually started a few weeks later, in August,
after I'd read the newspaper accounts of Troy, of Loganville,
of Grace. There probably *was* LSD, too, in the lemonade,
a willing enabler in the illusion, the *de*lusion I was creating for myself. I *wanted* to be Grace, to escape my own
past, my own future, and spend my life living hers. You
want that for me, too."

"I want the truth for you, Anastasia. Whatever that truth
may be."

"But you believe I might be Grace."

"I believe you *are* Grace. It would be a simple matter,

a single phone call, to resolve the issue of when your symptoms first appeared. You sought medical attention shortly after you awakened. I feel fairly confident those records would confirm that the headaches and coldness began in July. I'm also convinced that you'd stopped following the news *before* the revelations about Troy. According to Callie, you didn't realize, until the copies of *People* appeared, that the story Erin was telling was true."

"My head was hurting so much that day. I probably wasn't listening as I should have been."

"You were listening, Anastasia, to your girls. You'd never *not* listen no matter how you hurt. And moments later, despite how cold and aching you were, you assumed—quite ferociously, I might add—the solemn responsibility of protecting my niece. I was there, remember?"

I remember you, she thought. Most of all I remember *you*.

"There was nothing in the news, Anastasia, that would have made you want to become Grace. Not in July, not in · August, not anytime until this week. Only a handful of people knew before this week that Grace Alysia Quinn had survived the Yuletide blaze. Her loved ones knew. Garek McIntyre knew. And Grace knew. *You* knew."

He was telling her, so gently, that her wishing, wondering, wanting fantasy was true.

Her left hand, which had been nesting within his, took flight, joining her right, which had fluttered away earlier—and not returned. Both hands touched her face, her cheeks, which were rosy still, blooming still, even though she and Pierce no longer touched.

And Anastasia didn't tremble without his touch, did not quake.

"Your search for Grace began long before July," Pierce continued. "You'd been looking for her, remembering her, for years."

"Years?"

"Since you were fifteen at least, and maybe long before that. But certainly when you were fifteen and your false destiny of madness not gladness was revealed. The Grace within you knew it wasn't true, and began to assert herself with singing. With song. The two were linked, you told me. The disclosure of your diagnosis and your discovery that you could sing."

"Yes," she murmured. "They were."

I have to sing, she'd told him on the Island. I *have* to. *The Passion of Grace Alysia Quinn.*

She was a pensive Grace Alysia Quinn at this moment, reflective, thoughtful, not denying, not disbelieving, but not believing either.

Wishing, wondering, wanting—but not knowing.

"You've been identified as Grace by the one man on the planet empowered to make such a designation."

"Garek McIntyre?"

"That's right. Garek McIntyre."

"He has *proof*?"

"He's not requiring anything, Anastasia, beyond what information he already has. I don't know what that information is, although I'm sure it's detailed in the file. I do know that Garek is persuaded by it."

"Information," she echoed. "Circumstantial evidence, don't you think, not proof?"

"Circumstantial evidence can be compelling," ex-prosecutor Rourke assured. One could send a man to prison for his life if the circumstances were right, or, when compelling, even to his death. But was circumstantial evidence enough to convince a lost princess she was found? Or to persuade a trapped shadow she was finally free? Not this princess. Not this shadow. "There may be fingerprints on the coins, the cosmetics case, maybe both. Prints belonging to Carolyn or Troy. If so, that would be proof."

"Would *have been* proof. Any prints on the coins would have been erased long ago. I'd held them so often, as if I was holding my mother, touching her, needing to . . . and last July, or August, I polished them, needing to, wanting them suddenly to be shining and bright. I cleaned the cosmetics case at the same time, washed it, scrubbed it, inside and out. That sounds like destroying evidence, doesn't it? As if I knew Grace was alive and that I *wasn't* her?"

"That sounds," Pierce countered gently, "like someone who has nothing to prove. Which you don't, Anastasia. The burden of proof is on Garek, not you. And he's met that burden at its very highest standard—certainty beyond a shadow of a doubt." But the princess and her shadow doubted still. "The next step is for you to read the file. It's simply a matter of forwarding it from my e-mail to yours. May I?"

"Yes. Thank you."

Anastasia's slumbering computer was awakened with a

single keystroke by him, and *to* him, his face, from the eligible bachelor issue of *Mile High* magazine. She'd accessed it on-line, he imagined, and with a right click of her mouse had set it as her desktop wallpaper.

"This week," she confessed quietly, "as I read about Grace and my headaches were virtually constant and I felt so very cold, it helped me to look at you. I felt better when I did, better, warmer, safer."

Better, warmer, safer, Pierce mused. Anastasia was all of those now. Without him.

She'd done it herself, by acknowledging the wondering, wanting, wishing—and, with that acknowledgment, forging with the shadow at least a gentle truce.

"I'm glad." Pierce smiled even as he was aching, wishing, wanting *what*? Precariousness for her still? Such desperateness that she'd call him, as she had tonight, when his computer-screen image wasn't nearly enough? When she needed him to touch, hold her, make love to her?

Anastasia was warmer, safer, better. Without him.

But she was shimmering, shimmering, *for* him, because of him, as if in some way, in *every* way, he was responsible for the warmer, better, safer she felt—and responsible as well for the fantasy of Grace that might just be true.

As he typed the commands that would retrieve his e-mail from the electronic ether, Pierce Rourke set the record straight.

"Garek would have found you, Anastasia. Whether or not you'd ever sipped a glass of tainted lemonade, or moved to Denver, or dreamed about the Island. Giselle, who you knew as Gigi, would have read *People,* contacted Garek,

223

and tonight in Boston someone would have arrived, as I did, to tell you that Grace had been found. It would have happened, no matter what. Without the headaches, the coldness, the silence, the dream. And, Anastasia, it would have happened, no matter what, without me."

"But—"

"There. I've forwarded the file." He looked from the monitor to her. "Do you mind if I read it, too?"

"No, *of course* I don't mind. But I don't understand what you were just saying, *why* you were saying it."

"Because," he said softly, "it's true. And it was something I wanted to say before I left."

"You're leaving?"

"I don't think you're going to get cold again. Do you?"

"No. I don't. But . . ."

"Nothing has changed, Anastasia. Not for me. I want us, you, whoever you are." For better, for worse, in madness, in gladness, till death do us part. There it was. He would marry her this minute. Liam Pierce Rourke was in that deep, that committed, that certain, that involved. *But.* "I believe you are Grace, which means for you everything is about to change. Your future, your choices, very possibly your dreams."

"I . . ."

"Don't know?" Pierce ached, smiled. "How could you know? But you will know, in time. Take your time, Anastasia, and take care."

Moments later, Pierce stepped into a night that shed far warmer tears than the one he'd last known—a flood of raindrops so heated, so searing, that the ice rink that was Denver had melted away.

He made it home in no time.

Warmer, safer.

But not better.

EIGHTEEN

*G*iselle had spent the night imagining the moment when Garek would step into her room and they'd be alone. Together. With destiny.

She'd known in her imaginings that their dawn, *this* dawn, would be silver not black. The drapes in her lake-view suite weren't as occlusive as his. But the faint light would be all right for his sightless eyes, the glaring brilliance having faded, and the pewter glow of falling snowflakes would feel, did feel, like the mists, the magic, of Venice.

She'd known his hair would be shower damp, as hers was, long, lustrous, shining, clean. And that he would look more pale, more thin, after his all-night paroxysms of relief and pain. His eyes would be dark-circled, as hers were,

226

from lack of sleep. But they would glitter, and oh the blue was glittering, with desire.

With love.

Giselle had failed, however, to imagine the cane, the slender white antenna that had enabled Garek to find his way to her. He hadn't needed his cane last night. In his home. Nor, she thought, when he traveled by elevator from penthouse to work.

But the remainder of the time and in the rest of the world, the loner depended on his cane, trusted it, and with its help became his own eyes.

Garek would have needed his cane every step of the way on his journey to Carmel. And upon his arrival in the charming village by the sea, he'd have charted with his cane every foreign inch of darkness, learning it, hating it, knowing it, adjusting to it . . . so that he might date her, court her, if she was interested still.

"Tell me what you're thinking," he whispered in the silvery mist. "I can't quite see, and I'm a little afraid to guess."

"How much I love you."

Relief, with rescue, touched his beloved face.

Relief, with joy.

"I love you, Giselle. More than I ever believed it was possible for me to love."

His eyes, sightless and glittering, had never been so blue. And they told her, as if they saw, as if they knew, that she'd never been more beautiful than she was on this snowy dawn for him.

They'd never touched, these lovers. Garek hadn't dared

touch her in Venice. He'd have never let her go. And last night had been Grace's time, Grace's destiny, not theirs.

But as his cane fell away, and as if he was perfectly sighted in this magical light, his hands—his fingertips—met hers in midair. Caressed hers. Cherished. Kissed.

Only fingertips kissed at first, with wonder, with discovery. Then needing more, as lovers do, their fingers touched, pressing close, and closer, then their palms, closer still. Then gently yet insistently, persuasively, Garek parted her fingers with his, and their hands clasped, joined, became one.

It would have been enough, this silent touching, this quiet joy, this relief, this rescue, at dawn. More than enough, if it was all that was ever meant to be.

But the silvery light permitted much more.

Their lips met, caressed, discovered.

Tasted.

Garek tasted like desire to her, and fire at midnight and moonglow at dawn. And Giselle tasted like starlight to him, and rainbows of snowflakes and snowfalls of joy.

And they tasted, to each other, like love. Most of all love.

"Are you afraid?"

"Afraid, Garek?"

"Because of Armande. It wouldn't be surprising for you to be uncertain, to have memories, to have fear."

It was not, Giselle realized, an impromptu concern. This worry, so gentle for her, had been with him throughout the night, preventing sleep even in the rare moments, the respite moments, when he might have drifted off.

"What happened with Armande, what I did then, had nothing to do with making love. I've never made love,

Garek. Maybe that should scare me. But it doesn't, not with you."

"Because," he said softly, "you think I know what I'm doing. But I don't, Giselle. I've never made love before, either."

"Are you afraid?"

"Me? Afraid? Never." His smile was wry, sexy, tender. And he said, so tenderly, "But am I terrified? You bet."

"Me too," she confessed. "Terrified, Garek, but not afraid."

"I thought the kissing was going fairly well."

"I thought so, too."

It went well again, the kissing, the discovering—so well in the silvery mist where all magic was permissible, and where destiny and desire had become one, that they needed more, needed everything, needed all.

"Should you be doing this?"

"I beg your pardon?"

"This soon after the arteriogram? The femoral bleed?"

He laughed softly, moaned gently. "Giselle? I'm not going to bleed, and I can't get any more blind. If I don't make love to you soon, however, *very* soon, I may well die."

"Oh."

"Oh," he echoed, smiling. Then solemnly, and in the same words he'd spoken in Venice, Garek McIntyre whispered, "I've been waiting, my love. So patiently. But it's my time now. Our time. Isn't it?"

And it was, this snowy dawn that was their destiny.

It was time for love. For loving. For them.

At last.

NINETEEN

*T*hey could have lived forever, loved forever, in Giselle's bedroom. In Giselle's bed. Loving, sleeping, loving, talking, loving, smiling, loving, loving.

"Garek?" She would whisper, did whisper, again and again. "I'm interested *still*."

It wasn't desperate, their loving. Urgent at times, needy and wanting. But not desperate. Never desperate. They were where they belonged. Together.

It was where, they promised each other as they loved, they would always be.

Garek and Giselle were mindful, even as they loved, of the destinies that weren't nearly as certain as theirs. Just as Garek had been mindful the night before.

230

He'd checked his e-mail during the restless respites when he couldn't possibly sleep, and between frenzied paroxysms of pain, he'd sent an update to Olympia, a recap of the evening as it pertained to Grace.

There had been a middle-of-the-night e-mail from Pierce. Anastasia—Grace—had been told, the message said, and she'd accepted the revelation, the possibility of its truth, with thoughtful calm. It was as positive a message as could have been hoped. Yet Pierce's message had felt a little sad to Garek. Even the electronic voice that read it to him had sounded sad.

Giselle and Garek awaited further messages, even as they loved. Garek's pager would sound if any arrived. But it didn't sound, hadn't as of eight that night, when he carrying her suitcase and she carrying his cane, they'd returned to his penthouse.

Four hours later, at midnight, the e-mail from Anastasia arrived.

Giselle read it aloud, beginning as it did, with Anastasia's gracious thank-yous to both of them. She thanked Gigi for caring for the lost little girl she had been—whether that desperate little girl had been Anastasia or Grace—and, whether she was Anastasia or Grace, she thanked Garek for his compassionate search.

She didn't know, she confessed, if she was Grace.

She remembered Gigi. *Anastasia* remembered Gigi. But before that? Nothing. Neither fiery terror nor ferocious love.

Neither the monster Troy, nor the mother Mary Beth.

How could a mother who'd been so loved be so forgotten?

Yes, Anastasia's e-mail asserted, there were some *coincidences*. She'd been having headaches and inexplicable chilliness for the past six months. And she'd moved to Denver because it had felt right, felt necessary, that she do so.

And she *did* sing, loved to, needed to. At weddings. And she always made certain, in advance, that she'd be singing unobserved. But that had never felt like *modesty*. Rather, she'd always thought, it had been because intruding herself, a stranger, into the celebration seemed wrong.

She'd read with great interest, but no memory, of the afternoons Grace had spent at the Loganville library listening to fairy tales read aloud by Mrs. Bearce. In her own book club, for the third-grade class at Hazel Traphagen's School for Girls, the upcoming selections were always introduced, at librarian Anastasia Finch's suggestion, with the fairy tale beginning "Once upon a time."

And, she confessed, Jace Colton's Christmas Eve remembrance of Grace washing carrots for Santa's soaring flock *had* evoked . . . something. Rudolph always got three carrots, Grace had explained to him. Since it was Rudolph who led the way through the dark winter skies. The other reindeer, she'd told Jace, each got two.

Grace's earnest pronouncement sounded, *felt*, very familiar to Anastasia. She had no memory, however, of ever having made it herself.

But she was definitely enchanted by flying reindeer; had

232

been enchanted since her memories began. She'd even purchased this past Christmas a collection of reindeer mugs from Hallmark. The soaring creatures, in fanciful pastels, had been painted by Julia Hayley Colton. Jace's wife.

That meant nothing, of course. More *and pure* coincidence.

Anastasia acknowledged Carolyn Logan's unequivocal identification of her, and agreed that the photo-booth incident with Giselle *was* suggestive, and it was quite possible, she admitted, that she was twenty-nine not thirty-one. It wasn't until college that she'd stopped seeming younger than her classmates; physically, although not emotionally, less mature.

And, she conceded, the name Anastasia Finch made sense, given the cruelty and grandiosity of Troy. And, and, and, *but* she'd destroyed their four best chances of proof: the three coins and the cosmetics case.

Might there be something else? she wondered. Some other chance at *certainty*?

The substance of Anastasia's e-mail ended there. She repeated her gracious thank-yous, and promised to be diligent in her ongoing quest to remember something, *anything*, and she agreed, as their cover letter had proposed, that nothing, not the slightest suggestion of hope, should be shared with Grace's loved ones—yet.

"There may be another chance at proof," Garek said when Giselle had finished reading. Her voice had sounded sad, he'd thought as she'd read to him. As sad, he'd thought, as the electronic voice that had read the message from Pierce.

"Really, Garek?"

"There's really a chance, yes. Slim but real. If it happens to pay off, however, it will be definitive. I'll make some calls as soon as it's a reasonable hour to do so and set something up for tomorrow."

Tomorrow. Monday. The roadways *would* be passable. The main thoroughfares. Although, as of a late-night newscast they'd watched—listened to—expressly for the forecast, it would still be best for those who could stay at home until Tuesday to do so. But not everyone could.

"Your final MRI's tomorrow."

"And," he said, "a battery of end-of-protocol tests that may well keep me at the hospital the entire day."

"Keep *us* at the hospital the entire day."

Garek smiled. "It wouldn't be us, Giselle. Not together. It would be you, waiting somewhere, and me having tests somewhere else. Besides, your mission should you choose to accept it . . ."

It was a rescue mission, to which she responded with an enthusiastic yes.

There was nothing she'd rather do on a snowy Monday morning . . . except, of course, being *interested still* in him.

TWENTY

*H*e was in the cottage when she called. Wide-awake, at four that Sunday afternoon, but dreaming.

"It's me, Liam. Anastasia . . . and maybe, maybe Grace."

"Hello, Anastasia, and maybe, maybe Grace."

"I sent you a copy of the e-mail I sent to Garek and Giselle. Did you . . . ?"

"Get it?" *Read it? Memorize it? Listen in the electronic silence for the hope of a song?* "Yes. I did. Have you heard back?"

"Giselle called. To say hello mostly. Hello again. She's very nice. Well, of course you know that. She did say that Garek's trying to think of another way, *any* way, to find

235

conclusive proof. But, she said, I really shouldn't count on it."

"Do you agree?"

"Rationally, logically, yes."

"You sound good," Pierce said softly.

"I am good. *Better.* The headaches and coldness really *are* gone. I'm sure of it."

"That in itself feels like proof, doesn't it?"

"Yes. It does. A little. Sometimes a lot."

"What about your dream, Anastasia?" *Is it gone as well? Even though I'm here, in the cottage, looking at it still?*

"I don't know about the dream. I haven't slept since I saw you. I haven't even tried. But that's why I'm calling now." *Come sleep with me, Liam. Come dream with me.* "I'm going to bed soon, hopefully to sleep until morning, at which point I'm going to Loganville. If it was really my home, a place where I was so happy and loved, it seems, despite the amnesia, that something might feel familiar to me there."

"I agree." *Your joyful heart prints will be everywhere.* "And because I believe you are Grace, I feel very certain you'll find that something."

With that quiet assertion, that gentle confidence, silence fell. Too soon, Pierce thought, ached, she would say goodbye, to sleep, to dream. *Sleep well, Anastasia. Dream—*

"Will you be with me when I do? Or, Liam, when I *don't?*"

"You want me to come with you to Loganville?"

"Yes." *Please.* "If tomorrow's not good for you, we could make it another day."

Architect Rourke had scheduled for the following day a series of meetings about the lake of ice within Carillon Square. Essential meetings, during which to the assembled electricians and engineers, Pierce would explain patiently, and unyieldingly, that the fountain of violets *would* twirl separately from the solitary skater, and that since the ballet of glass and water would be set to music—yes, that detail *was* new—the nozzles wreathed by violet blossoms would need to move as well, and that there would be track lighting beneath the ice, yes, *beneath*, and . . .

"Tomorrow's fine, Anastasia. And I want to come."

"And skate with me?"

"Skate?"

"On the Loganville lake. I got skates for both of us today. I measured your shoe prints on my carpet and was assured by the sporting-goods skate expert that the size I bought for you was right."

Pierce smiled, ached, hoped. "I'll skate with you, Anastasia." *Gladly. With gladness.* "Sure I will."

I will skate with you, sing with you.

Love you.

$\mathcal{G}$arek's penthouse phone sounded as Giselle was preparing to leave for her rescue mission for Anastasia. For Grace.

It was ten o'clock Monday morning. Garek had been gone for three hours, and although he'd called when he'd reached the hospital, an uneventful trip thanks to an experienced Wind Chimes chauffeur, he didn't anticipate being able to call again until early afternoon.

But maybe there'd been a break between the MRI, the EEG, or one of the many other end-of-protocol tests his physicians had planned.

Or maybe Garek had simply told his doctors he was *taking* a break. Maybe he'd seen, despite his darkness, her silent worry. Maybe he'd read, from his blackness, her desperate thoughts.

Her silent worry: What aren't you telling me, Garek? Her desperate thoughts: What secrets are you keeping even as we've promised, as we've loved, to share *every* truth?

Giselle hadn't posed her anxious questions. She'd waited, trusted, *believed*. Garek would tell her without prompting. He *would*.

And now the phone was ringing.

"Hello?"

"Giselle?"

"Yes?"

"My name is Kathleen. You don't know me. You may not even know of me. Garek and I were married once."

"Yes. I do know."

"Oh. Good. Then I'll just cut to the chase. Garek's not there, is he? The Towers' doorman said he left early this morning and had yet to return."

"That's right. He's not here."

"I need to talk to you, Giselle. I'm *not* a crazed ex-wife. I promise. At least not anymore. There's something you need to know about Garek. Something he *needs* you to know. It's terribly important. Really. May I come up?"

"I was on my way down." *What aren't you telling me,
Garek?* "There's an errand I have to run." *What secrets are
you keeping even as we've promised to share every truth?* "It
shouldn't take long. It's just a matter of dropping something off about a mile away. I'd planned to walk, but maybe
I can find a cab."

"What if I walk with you?"

"Oh. Yes." *Please.* "That would be great."

*G*arek's ex-wife was beautiful. Inside and out. Giselle liked
her at once.

Kathleen was *not* a vengeful courtesan. No Venetian
dagger lurked beneath her downy parka, nor were there
daggers in her eyes.

Talking while walking wasn't possible, not in any mean-
ingful way. The snowy sidewalks were crowded, and treacherous.

Once Giselle's errand was complete, her—small—part
of the rescue mission accomplished, they found a Star-
bucks, hot chocolate, and a corner table.

"I'm really *not* a crazed ex-wife," Kathleen reiterated before she began. "And what I need to tell you is about the
present, not the past. But a little past history is necessary,
I think, so that you'll understand why I called you today.
So, let's see. I guess Garek's hotel room in Geneva is the
place to start. I hadn't accompanied him to Geneva. We
were separated at the time. But the moment I heard what
happened in the Balkans, I flew to Switzerland. So there

I was, in his hotel room, waiting for him to become stable enough to be transferred from the battlefield hospital,
praying that such a time would even come. At some point
during that excruciating wait I decided to pack his things,
which included a boarding pass from a flight from Venice,
as well as a brochure from the Festival of Masks. I was in
a blur, frantic about him. But even if I'd been *totally* focused I would have concluded that once he realized he'd
be in Geneva during Carnivale, he would have taken the
opportunity to see your work. I'd even have been envious
that he'd had the chance to do so, and that I *hadn't*, but
I'd have been delighted that he'd kept the brochure to
show to me."

Were it not for Kathleen's assertion that this was about
the present, not the past, Giselle would have interjected
that her totally focused conclusion would have been correct. But Giselle didn't interject.

"In any event, my focus was on Garek's survival, and
nothing else. And finally he was transferred. He was still
near death, his survival very much in doubt. But he was
concerned about another life. A *potential* life. Was I pregnant, he wondered, with his child? He was so desperate
to know that I almost lied. But I didn't. Maybe I somehow sensed that the answer he wanted so desperately was
no, not yes. And *no* was the truth. I wasn't pregnant. I'm
not sure why he even thought that I might be."

"Because when you'd spoken with him just before his
trip to Geneva, you'd sounded like the old Kathleen and
more, something radiant and glowing and new."

"He heard a lot more than I ever gave him credit for,"

Kathleen said quietly. "Even before he became blind. What was new, Giselle, what I'd realized, was that I was in love with him. It wasn't supposed to happen, not to me, not ever. But it had. That's what I was going to tell him. What I *did* tell him. He didn't need to love me in return. I knew he didn't and never would. But if he'd just permit me to acknowledge my love, and live it, I'd be one very happy wife. He didn't have to change. I didn't *want* him to. But he'd already changed, he told me. Even before his injury, before his blindness, he'd decided he wanted a divorce. After hearing my confession, he was committed to moving forward as quickly as was legally possible. He'd never love me as I should be loved, he said, as I *deserved* to be. Never, not wounded or whole, sighted or blind. I wondered if he'd met someone. If he, too, had fallen in love. But surely I would have known. She would have been at his bedside in Switzerland, and for all those months in the hospital here. I would have seen her, met her, befriended her. I was there, as his friend, with Olympia. Even after our divorce."

"And do you see him sometimes still?"

"Yes. Sometimes. You might think *often*, since I live and work in the Towers, too. But it's a big building, and we're living our own lives, our separate lives. I call him from time to time, and he calls me. We were always pretty good at talking to each other. Openly. Honestly. He was openly, honestly furious when I confronted him three months ago with an anonymous letter I'd received."

"An anonymous letter?"

"Sent to me at WCHM. From a listener who knew we'd been married. I haven't the foggiest idea who sent the let-

241

ter, nor could it matter less. What matters is that the information in the letter was true. Garek was, in fact, planning to consent to a surgery, a *neuro*surgery, that had a ten percent chance of success *at best*. Success being defined as restoring his vision *and* leaving him alive to enjoy it. On the other side, the ninety percent side, was failure. Defined as death. The ninety percent being optimistic, in the letter writer's opinion. He or she placed the chance of failure, *death*, at a hundred percent. It was suicide pure and simple. Couldn't I, as Garek's ex-wife, persuade him to dismiss the notion out of hand?"

"Which you could and did."

"Which I *couldn't*. And *didn't*. Garek was furious in a way I'd never seen. I'd never seen fury, even anger, from him at all. But I saw it then. Cold, *ice*-cold, and stark, and *dark*. It was his life, he said. *His*. What right did I, did anyone, have to tell him how to live it? Or *not* live it? I was to tell *no one* what I'd discovered. He was most concerned, I knew, about Olympia. She has her own hospital source—who, quite obviously, hadn't heard about the brain surgery being planned. I would have known if Olympia knew. As would Garek. He didn't want Olympia to worry, and she *would* have. He hadn't wanted me to worry, either, I realized. He just wanted to have the surgery without anyone knowing or caring in advance. If he died, he died, and no one, not Olympia, not I, would feel responsible for not having intervened."

"But you did intervene," Giselle insisted. "And you convinced him."

"No, Giselle, I *didn't*. That's why I'm telling you this

242

now. I'd have told you three months ago if I'd known about you then. I *could* have known. The clues, in retrospect, were there. Beginning with the boarding pass. It was a souvenir *obviously*, sentimental, important, not something the Garek I knew would ever have saved. Then there was the day I confronted him about the surgery. We were in his living room, and he was looking at *Venetian Dawn*, staring as if he was seeing it clearly. *Perfectly*. As if he'd *willed* himself to see. It was very powerful, and even a little frightening. The intensity of the emotion, of the *wanting*. What he wanted so powerfully, I decided, was to see. But now I realize that what he wanted, so powerfully, was to see *you*. It all came together this morning. The Towers' doorman said that he'd met you on Friday, when Olympia was showing you the codes to Garek's penthouse. You and Garek met in Venice, and then he was injured, and did you even *know*?"

"No. I didn't. Not until last Thursday night."

"I'm so *sorry* I didn't figure it out sooner. I would have called you. Who cares how furious Garek would have been? You could have been with him *all this time*."

"Thank you," Giselle murmured to the woman who, as Garek had forecast in Venice, would be amazed but accepting of their love, and who would wish him, wish them, all the best. It was true. Even though, in the meantime, Kathleen had fallen in love with Garek herself.

"Thank *you*, Giselle. And thank *heaven* you're here. You love him, don't you? And he loves you?"

"Yes, and yes. Thank heaven I'm here?"

"You can stop him from killing himself. Maybe you already have, just by being here. Except . . ."

"*Except?*"

"Garek wants to see you *so much.*"

He does see me, Giselle thought. He sees me, knows me, reads my thoughts, my heart, even in darkness. And it's enough, isn't it? Enough *for him?* "It's been three months, Kathleen, since you found out about the surgery. He's clearly decided not to have it."

"No. That's *not* clear. The surgery was never going to happen until the research study was complete. They knew three months ago the infusions weren't going to reverse his blindness, not on their own. But that didn't mean they weren't doing *some* good, something that might improve the possibility of surgical success. The neurosurgeons wanted to operate the moment the protocol was complete. Which would have been soon. Any day now. But thank heaven, too, for Grace Alysia Quinn. Garek didn't tell me, but I'm quite sure it's true, that he wouldn't have the surgery, wouldn't let himself die, until she was found. I'd been hoping, perversely, that would never happen. But now that you're here, Giselle . . ."

I'm here, and Grace is found, I've brought her to him, and it doesn't matter that we've promised to tell each other every truth. Garek is keeping secrets still, living his life, choosing his life, alone. As always.

TWENTY-ONE

"*I* really *would* be afraid to have children."

Anastasia's statement ended the silence that had traveled with them since Pierce had picked her up at the Canterbury at 8:45. An hour ago.

It had been a shimmering silence, violet fragrant and hopeful, filled with soft smiles and gentle glances.

And now, two miles from Loganville, came Anastasia's quiet words, her emphatic assertion, as if this so-important topic was something she and Pierce had already discussed, had *been* discussing . . . as if, in the shimmering silence, they'd been singing a most glorious duet. a song of love between a wishing, willing, wanting bridegroom and his courageous bride.

245

"Unless," that wishing man said softly, "you were certain you were Grace."

"Yes. It would be so unfair, to a daughter, to be born with the genes of madness. And unfair, too, for a son to watch his mother go mad and die. Even adoption would be unfair. And yet . . ."

"And yet?"

"You'd be such a wonderful . . . oh, no. *No.* I can't believe—" Anastasia stopped. Abruptly. With alarm, and despair where there'd been such hope.

Abruptly, but not recklessly, Pierce pulled to the side of the road.

He looked at her and smiled, made himself smile. For her.

"You can't believe that I'd be a wonderful father? Was that what you were starting to say?"

"What? No. *No.* You would be a *wonderful* father. Of course you would be. It's just that . . ."

"Talk to me, Anastasia." *Talk to me. Sing with me.*

"It was a dream. A *dream.* But it felt so real. I guess I awakened this morning believing it had been. If this isn't proof of madness—"

"We were on the Island."

"Yes."

"Discussing our future."

"*Yes.*"

"That doesn't sound like madness, Anastasia. Unless, in the light of day, the dream has lost its appeal. Has it?"

Her blue eyes, which had clouded with her despair, became bright for him, clear for him.

"No," she said. "It hasn't." Her eyes, so clear, saw with wondrous clarity the glittering brilliance of his, the glowing emerald in the forest, the light of happiness her confession—the truth—had evoked. The truth, and yet . . .

"Talk to me, Anastasia."

"It was all *so easy* in the dream. It didn't matter whether I was Anastasia or Grace."

"It doesn't matter. It never has. There was, I take it, a little gladness in your dream?"

"So much gladness."

"Did we marry?"

"We . . . planned to."

"We will, Anastasia, on the Island. In front of the people we love. But I'd like a far more private ceremony first. Here. Now. Before Loganville."

Before Loganville. While she was still Anastasia, and might never be Grace.

"Marry me, Anastasia. Marry me now."

He hadn't been touching her. Nor did he. But he made for his songbird a welcoming nest of his hands. This was a new nest, this home that sang, and different from the nest he'd made for her on Friday night. She didn't need this gentle sanctuary. She could fly on her own.

But the nest was there if she wanted it, a place to dream if she wished it, a home where, forever, she could sing.

And she wanted the home he made for her.

She did.

Her hands curled within his, and when he spoke, when he could, there was joy.

"I, Liam Pierce, take you, Anastasia Grace, for my wife, for my life, for my forever."

"Liam," she whispered. "Pierce." Then softly, with song, "I, Anastasia Grace, take you, Liam Pierce, for my life, for my love, for my forever."

They kissed slowly. Gently. Chastely. In these moments before Loganville. They would make love later, after, forever after, on the Island, in their cottage, with its view of her dream.

Later. After. When they had found in Loganville the delicate heart prints of a shadow . . . the delicate shadows of a heart.

*G*arek McIntyre was in the neurosurgical ICU.

At least, the pink-coated volunteer at the patient information desk informed a breathless Giselle, that was where his bed was. The volunteer had no way of knowing where the patient was at that moment. In neuroradiology. In the operating room.

Or, a thought screamed within Giselle, in the morgue.

The screaming thought, ungovernable and macabre, was the ghoulish culmination of the thoughts that had taunted as she'd run through once-rainbowed snow.

Garek hated his blindness. He'd told her as much. He'd simply neglected to mention that he hated the blackness of his world more than he cherished the brilliance of their love.

And he hadn't needed to mention it on this morning.

He'd created a diversion for her, a rescue mission of her own, so that he could, without interference, go ahead with his plans.

As he had every right to do. It was—as, with anger, he'd told Kathleen—*his* life, *his* choice, *his* darkness, *his* death.

But what was it that Garek had told Giselle about his careless mistake, from caring too much, in the Balkans? Carelessness was bad enough, he'd said. Inexcusable. But the inexcusable became the unforgivable when you risked *other* lives . . . when, in your risk-taking, you took others with you.

You're risking my life, Garek! her heart had cried as she'd raced through smoke-gray snow. You'll take me with you if you die. I don't forgive you, Garek. I won't forgive you.

Yes I do, yes I would, yes I will.

The neurosurgical ICU was on the seventh floor. The unit's clerk, positioned at the entrance, confirmed that Mr. McIntyre was a patient *and* was in his room.

And, after a brief consultation with her computer, the clerk confirmed that Giselle was a permitted visitor.

A nurse named Brian escorted Giselle to Garek. It was a substantial journey. The unit was vast, and Garek was at its farthest reach. It was also a shadowed journey.

The lights were low, as if dimmed for romance, for romantics, for lovers. Or for patients—lovers turned patients—for whom bright lights might provoke seizures, or worse.

Dr. Clayton would want to speak with Giselle, Brian announced when their journey was complete. He'd put in a page. In the meantime, it would be best if Giselle remained outside Garek's room.

So the glass sculptress saw her lover, her Garek, through glass. Her Garek.

Garek's Garek.

He was motionless save for the ventilator breaths. His head was swathed in layers of white, a turban of gauze laced with wires—which probed his brain?—and was anchored, his *head* was anchored, by gigantic silver tongs.

It looked like torture to Giselle.

It was torture. For her.

And for him? She strained to hear a soft moan. Some proof, *that* proof, that Garek wasn't beyond torture . . . that he was wounded but alive, injured but fighting, screaming, weeping, hurting, praying.

There was no sound. No human one. No animal one. Merely the rhythmic breaths of the ventilator, and rhythmically, too, the beeps from the cardiac monitor overhead.

"Giselle? I'm sorry, I didn't mean to startle you. Are you all right?"

The quiet voice, the female voice, had startled her. It sounded so loud, as quiet as it was, in this place of shadows where she'd been listening for a moan. And was she all right? *No.* But to the sympathetic woman in the crisp white coat and rumpled blue scrubs, Giselle replied, "Yes."

"Good. I'm Lucy Clayton. I was just about to call you when I got the page. Garek said you'd be returning to his penthouse about now. I guess he was able to reach you himself."

Reach me? You mean he tried? "How is he?"

"Miserable, I would imagine. I don't care what you've been trained to endure, being intubated and paralyzed while awake evokes—"

"He's awake?" *Paralyzed, but awake. Alive.* "Already?"

"He's never been asleep."

"I don't understand. You operated while he was awake?"

"I didn't operate at all. No one did. I'm beginning to think he *didn't* reach you."

"No. He didn't."

"Then let me reassure you, first, before I explain. The paralysis I mentioned is pharmacologic, intentional, and will entirely reverse. *We'll* reverse it tomorrow. Garek's okay, Giselle. Miserable, most likely, but okay."

"Thank you," she whispered.

"I didn't do anything. No one did. Except, possibly, you."

"Me?"

"You were with him this weekend. That much I know." Dr. Clayton smiled. "And in exactly that much detail. Over the course of your weekend together, Garek started seeing shapes."

"He did?"

"Yes, he did. He didn't tell you, because he believed it wouldn't last. But it did last, *and* there were dramatic changes on this morning's MRI. I'd been unalterably opposed to a surgical procedure that Garek and the neuro-surgeons had discussed. I'm a neuro-ophthalmologist, so I'm not averse to surgery, but what they were discussing seemed excessively dangerous and doomed to fail."

"So you sent a letter . . ."

"To Kathleen? Nope. That wasn't me. Although, as significant an ethical breach as it was, when Garek told me about it, I told him I heartily approved. That should give you some insight into how surprising it was for me—this morning—to be endorsing a surgical procedure after all. It would have been far more limited, hence less risky, though still risky, than the one previously discussed. And given the MRI findings, the chance of success had gone way up. I assumed Garek would go for it in a heartbeat. But, in a heartbeat, he said no. It's the first time in the nearly three years I've known him that Garek McIntyre actually gave a damn whether he lived or died. I don't need to know the details of your weekend, Giselle, to know that that's because of you."

Dr. Clayton paused, smiled, then continued, "We did a seventh infusion instead, from which, in a few hours, he'll need a seventh rescue. The infusion was selective, based on the MRI findings. It was best, safest, to have him intubated and paralyzed while we were doing that, and it continues to be best. By controlling his breathing, we're able to manipulate carbon-dioxide levels, which in turn allows us to manipulate the dilatation of arterioles in his visual cortex. We had to paralyze him so that he wouldn't fight the ventilator, which he would have done reflexively, his muscles would have, in physiologic response to the markedly abnormal CO_2."

"Is that usual?"

"Intubation with pharmacologic paralysis? In a neurosurgical unit, yes. In this one especially. Which is why we admitted him here. He's a little more conscious than your typical neurosurgery patient. But, since we want to increase his cerebral blood flow not diminish it, we're reluctant to sedate him. We're not going to. Which he knew, agreed to, in advance. But he's miserable. He *has* to be. He'll be far less miserable though, I feel quite certain, now that you're here. He really didn't want to proceed until he spoke with you. But we pushed him. *I* pushed him. The MRI changes were so impressive that the sooner we capitalized on them the better."

"The tongs, the wires . . ."

"The wires are electrodes, a bedside EEG, and, as barbarous as they look, the tongs are necessary to keep his head positioned exactly where it needs to be. I think we've wrapped enough gauze that the discomfort should be minimal."

"He can feel?"

"Yes. It's only his muscles that don't work. You probably have other questions?"

"May I be with him?"

"You bet."

TWENTY-TWO

"*H*i," she whispered. "Rumor has it you're wide-awake and miserable. *I love you.* Oh-oh, oops, that sounded a little emotional, didn't it? A little weepy. My mission, I decided, at least I *had* decided, was to keep you amazingly entertained for the next, oh, eighteen hours. With respites, I'd thought, during which I hoped you'd be able to sleep. But *I love you.*"

Giselle drew a steadying breath, which steadied very little. It was terrifying to see him so still. Even his eyelashes didn't flutter. Could not flutter.

"I was blind, you know. Before you. *I* was blind. You made me see, Garek McIntyre, all those years ago. *You made me see.* I saw Venice because of you, and the glass fires of Murano, that hope, that dream. And three years ago, because of you, I saw love. And now I'm living that love, living it, because of you. Thank you for loving me, my Garek, for loving us, for wanting us, for not risking us. *Thank you.*"

There was movement then, on his deathly still face, a gentle spill of glistening heat from beneath the motionless lashes, a flow of love from his heart to hers.

Giselle kissed the spilling warmth, the shimmering heat, and she tasted, as she kissed his tears, the man, the loner, who was alone no more, and who, this rescuer, had been rescued by love, and who, despite his blindness, was telling her that he could see, would see forever, the pastel fall of snowflakes . . . and the champagne rays of dawn.

*L*oganville was quaint, charming, beautiful. The kind of place where, it was so easy to imagine, a golden-haired girl would have been nourished, and would have flourished, with love.

It would have been easy to imagine, too, the places within the charming town where the girl had spent such happy years. No imagining would have been required, however, for anyone who'd visited the Finding Grace web site. All of Grace's favorite spots were there.

And the retracing of the joyful steps was made even easier, so easy, by the map that had been posted, and lovingly annotated, by Mrs. Bearce.

They followed that map, from Loganville General, where the photo booth had been, to Grace's preschool on South

Cherry, to the elementary school on Grand, to Dinah's home on Sycamore, to the library on Ponderosa, to Bluebird Lane, where Grace and Mary Beth had lived . . . and where, at the site of the house that had burned to ash, there had been ever since a beautifully landscaped park.

Anastasia and Pierce retraced the footsteps of Grace Alysia Quinn. Slowly. Reverently. Attentively. Expectantly.

And?

"There's nothing," she whispered, and whispered and whispered. "Nothing that's familiar to me in any way."

"We haven't been to the lake yet."

"No."

"Shall we?"

"I don't know. It's the last place, the final chance, and if there's nothing there . . ."

"Dr. Kline predicted that the amnesia would be permanent."

"I know." She smiled faintly, bravely. "And I also know that, like your brother-in-law, he's one of the very best."

"Thomas's mentor, in fact. Let's go to the lake, Anastasia. If nothing else, we still get to skate. Yes," he said softly, "we do."

And, my love, we still get to spend our lives together. Yes, he vowed fiercely, *we do.*

Pierce hadn't the slightest doubt that, photographs on the web site notwithstanding, Loganville Lake would look, feel, *be* the lake in her dream déjà vu.

But he was wrong.

The lake looked, on this Monday, exactly as in the web-

site photos—except that on this school day, without the
gaiety of skaters, the shining ice was quite desolate.

Quite without hope.

As she was.

Pierce saw her disappointment, and felt the deep ache
of his own. But for her, for them, he smiled.

"Let's try a little skating."

"We don't have to."

"Yes," he said. "We do."

Liam Pierce Rourke was a natural athlete, a natural lover,
a natural singer, and he would be, *he would be*, a natural
husband and father.

But he really couldn't skate.

And she really could.

After a few wobbling glides, Pierce let go of her hand.

She could survive without his touch. Both could survive
without touching—for a while.

Besides, Pierce realized, they were touching still.

He didn't know about the second skater Giselle planned
for *her* glass sculpture within *his* Carillon Square. The one,
since he'd been so unyielding in his vision, that would be
quite invisible . . . but who would be watching the ballerina he loved as she twirled amid violets and reached for
the moon.

Pierce was that second skater now, and she was spinning, the lost princess he loved, and twirling, the lovely
shadow within her, and they were feeling, both shadow
and princess, the heart prints of Loganville—at last.

She could have reached for the sky, his twirling skater,
as she reached for it in her dream.

But she was no longer that solitary skater.

She reached for him instead, a silent invitation of grace, from Grace, across the shimmering expanse of ice.

Come to me. Skate with me. Be with me. Always.

So he did, the natural athlete who could not skate. And when, hands joined and smiling, they twirled together in the middle of the lake, the natural husband and father—who could not skate—tripped just a little.

Just enough.

For, with that slight stumble, their gliding twirl halted precisely where it needed to, so that they could see in the distance the snowfield of her dream.

It made sense, they should have known, that it would have been a skater's vista, a skater's view, beheld when it was she who was the island in the center of a lake.

*A*nastasia needed no more proof than the heart prints she had found.

But there was more proof to come.

Giselle's mission, on that Monday in Chicago, had been to take her photo-booth photos to the forensics expert who'd studied—and catalogued—the fingerprints found on Dinah's.

Dinah's photos had been cluttered with prints, young and old, large and small, almost all of which had been identified.

Almost all. There was no way of knowing which, if any, of the remaining prints, pieces of same, belonged to Grace.

Not until Grace was found. And even then, a negative match would mean nothing, in fact was *likely*, given the many fingers that had touched Dinah's photos over the intervening years.

Garek hadn't wanted to ask Anastasia for her prints. She'd had doubts enough already. But with Giselle's photos the search could be done without Anastasia's knowing, and if there wasn't a match . . .

It was a tedious process. It had taken a while. Nine days. But at the end of those nine days, the forensics expert was able to show Garek, *show* Garek, the conclusive evidence he had found: the perfect match of tiny remnants, the bits of ridges, fragments of loops, and pieces of swirls.

Garek McIntyre had in turn shown his wife. His bride.

The following day, Giselle and Garek—and Olympia and her husband—flew to Denver for a wedding.

And what a wedding it was, on the island of snow and music and glass and dreams.

All the Loganville loved ones were there, including, from the Emerald City, Jace and Julia Colton, with their daughter Josie. And Carolyn Logan, though not strictly speaking a loved one, was invited, too. She wept at the invitation itself, and again, on the Island, when she felt the kindness with which she was received.

And all the Denver loved ones were there. Lilah and Edward, and Thomas and Val, and Melissa and Callie and Doug. And Dr. Kline and his wife. And, of course, the Peggys.

Every Peggy was invited to the wedding of their beloved

Miss Finch and Callie's wonderful Uncle Pierce. And every Peggy's family was invited, too, which meant six times eighteen invitations, less the multiple Peggys per family, plus faculty, plus staff—well, Val did the math.

And so they were wed, on their Island of dreams, and where, in her dreams, she'd seen a snowfield, on a sparkling night, that was the silken gown of a heavenly bride, and where crystal mountains, in a starlit blue, had glowed like proud parents in the velvet sky.

And on that night, when they were wed, amid the songs of the stars and the music of the moon, their parents, his and hers, looked down from the heavens . . . and smiled.

Katherine Stone is the author of sixteen novels, including *Thief of Hearts*, *Bed of Roses*, *Imagine Love*, *Pearl Moon*, and *Twins*. Her work has been translated into nineteen languages. A physician who now writes full time, she lives with her husband, novelist Jack Chase, in the Pacific Northwest. You can learn more about her novels by visiting her Web site at www.katherinestone.com.